"How much, Miss Warren?" Hugh Rydon asked tonelessly

Lindsay's heart gave a thump. This was all wrong...No surprise, no question, no demand for an explanation.

"Twenty thousand pounds," she answered evenly, and was ready to meet his disbelieving eyes when they lifted.

"Will you repeat that, please?" he asked in a voice that was like slivers of ice, contempt clear in his eyes.

Lindsay was shocked, but her eyes flashed angrily. "Oh, I think you heard me, Mr. Rydon. Your cousin Charles owes me twenty thousand pounds. And I'd prefer a company check. I've found personal ones have a tendency to bounce."

He glared at her and Lindsay glared back. Then, to Lindsay's incredulous fury, his eyes left her face to slide down over her body suggestively. "Are you pregnant, Miss Warren?"

EDWINA SHORE

just another married man

Harlequin Books

TORONTO • NEW YORK • LONDON
AMSTERDAM • PARIS • SYDNEY • HAMBURG
STOCKHOLM • ATHENS • TOKYO • MILAN

To Tina

Harlequin Presents first edition May 1989
ISBN 0-373-11172-X

Original hardcover edition published in 1988
by Mills & Boon Limited

CHAPTER ONE

MAGGIE'S telegram was typically Maggie—succinct and economical; her mother never wasted words or money if she could help it. 'Cheque bounced. Twice,' Lindsay read, and she kept staring at the three words as if they were in some strange language she couldn't understand. Only she did understand, because nothing could have been clearer than the fact that she and Maggie had been conned.

And then Lindsay wanted to laugh. Shock, she supposed scrunching the telegram fiercely into a tight little ball in her fist and ramming it into the pocket of her coat. Afterwards, it occurred to her that it was curious that she hadn't for one moment thought there must be some mistake about Charles' cheque . . . a bank error or something. Even without the word 'twice', indicating that Maggie had re-presented the cheque, Lindsay would have simply assumed the worst.

She moved across the room to the window and gazed down absently at the wintry bareness of the communal garden which ran along behind the fence of the hotel's scraggy backyard, and continued right down the length of the block. It looked freezing outside, and was near enough to

freezing inside as well, with the two bars of the
electric heater barely taking the chill off the shabby
little room. A shiver shot through her and Lindsay
huddled deeper into the heavy navy coat.

How could anyone think in this sort of cold
. . .? February in London. She had never
experienced anything like it: hands always half-
numb, the tip of her short, straight nose feeling like
ice . . . ears stinging, and now her brain seemed to
have gone into cold storage and was refusing to
function. She let out a sigh and watched the hiss of
breath mist up the patch of glass in front of her,
then, with a sudden, angry movement, pulled a
hand out of her pocket and scrawled 'Fool' on to
the misted glass. Naïve fools, that was what they
had been, she and Maggie, both.

'Ruytons, Lindsay, Ruytons! Imagine . . .'
Maggie had been thrilled to her back teeth—and
charmed out of a twenty-thousand-black opal
pendant like a child out of her candy. Shrewd, no-
nonsense Maggie, who had worked her way up
from the opal fields of Coober Pedy to run her own
opal wholesale business in Sydney . . . who prided
herself on being able to spot a conman at fifty paces,
hadn't stood a chance against Charles Rydon, nor
her own delicious vision of Maggie Warren supplying
gems to a jewellery house as famous as Ruytons of
London. 'Cartier and Tiffany's next, darling, mark
my words.' Maggie had been over the moon—with a
push from Charles.

Poor Maggie. Poor Maggie, nothing, Lindsay
thought grimly. Her own fantasies hadn't been any

more outlandish than her mother's: London . . .
setting Ruytons on its ear with her excitingly
different designs . . . winning the odd award . . .
And all based on a three-week acquaintanceship
with Charles Rydon. Well, a little more than that,
Lindsay had to admit . . . a flirtation, if not quite
romance, and a lot of fun, but she must have been
mad to have taken Charles' promises seriously. To
have taken *Charles* seriously. He had introduced
himself at the jewellery designers' exhibition in
Sydney where her own pendant with the fabulous
black opal had taken the top honours. He was a
very attractive man . . . tall, fair, boyishly good-
looking, with an air of lazy self-assurance and a
laid-back charm to go with it. The intensely blue
eyes had lit up with undisguised admiration as they
took her in—from the top of the sleek swirl of
honey-blonde hair . . . down the five foot nine of
her slim, lithe form in its black silk . . . to the tips
of her tanned feet in the evening sandals.

Lindsay was twenty-four, and hadn't come
down in the last shower where men were
concerned. She was an attractive woman and used
to men finding her so, and she wasn't given to
being bowled over by a good-looking man doing a
line. But what had bowled her over—flattered her
out of her mind—was that Charles Rydon, whose
family had owned Ruytons for generations, and
who now ran the famous firm, had thought her
pendant the most exciting piece of design work
he'd seen in years.

The romance . . . fliration—whatever—between

them during the three weeks of his stay in Australia had been a romance with the magic name of Ruytons for Lindsay. She had been bewitched, beguiled, enjoying the wining and dining, and, yes, Charles' romantic overtures too. All part of the act; she knew that now.

At the time, it had seemed perfectly natural that he should buy the black opal pendant to take back to London with him to enter in a coming exhibition . . . an annual charity function, Charles explained, at which a number of the top jewellers exhibited a selective range. Commissions invariably flowed on, and she'd have commissions galore waiting for her when she reached London, he had promised her.

Lindsay had already been planning to come to England in about four months' time, and Charles had been delighted when she'd told him, immediately talking about her joining Ruytons . . . setting up a new line featuring opals which Lindsay would design using the best stones her mother could supply.

How could Charles possibly have failed after all that?

Lindsay didn't wait the four months, and, while she didn't exactly catch the next plane to London, she left a week later, the lure of Ruytons too tempting to put off a moment longer than could be helped. And Maggie had encouraged her for all she was worth.

Charles hadn't given her his address in London, and he was ex-directory, too, Lindsay had found when she wanted to telephone him on her arrival.

That had been a week ago. She had booked into a cheap and, predictably, rather down-at-the-heel private hotel in Bayswater, and spent a breathlessly overawed weekend positively gawping around London before turning up at Ruytons on Monday morning, smiling to herself as she pictured Charles' surprise when she walked into his office.

He hadn't been in, which wasn't unduly surprising, but what Lindsay had found rather amazing was that nobody seemed to have any idea when he might be in—nor appeared at all interested. Her telephone calls during the following two days had produced the same vague non-information, and that was when Lindsay had begun to feel uneasy. It wasn't that Ruytons hadn't heard of him—obviously they had, yet Lindsay couldn't help gathering the impression that Charles Rydon was not quite who—what—she thought he was—or who he had led her to believe he was within the organisation.

Yesterday, Thursday, she had gone in again and asked to speak to someone in charge, determined to get some straight answers from somebody—and had, from the tall, elderly man who presented himself as the manager of the Gallery—Ruytons' term for their beautiful showroom. Mr Barlow had told her all she needed to know, to wit, that 'Mr Charles' did not run Ruytons, his cousin, Mr Hugh Rydon did; that 'Mr Charles' only 'dropped in' from time to time in his capacity as artistic consultant, whatever that meant; and to cap his interesting revelations, Mr Barlow had added in his

dry, precise voice that 'Mr Charles' was believed to
be in Paris with his wife this week, and could
anyone else help her?

'No, thank you,' Lindsay had said, very calmly,
and walked out, stunned at the outrageousness of
Charles' lies . . . fantasies . . . about himself.

Coming after all that, Maggie's telegram simply
blew the last of his credibility; small wonder
Lindsay had no trouble believing it, and yet,
somewhere at the back of her mind, she was
puzzled, because swanning about on the other side
of the world trying his hand at a bit of philandering
and attempting to impress 'the colonials' with his
importance was one thing; stealing a twenty-
thousand-pound opal was quite another, and
surely Charles couldn't be expecting to get away
with it . . .?

The knock on her door made Lindsay start.
Earlier in the week, every tap on the door had had
her anticipating Charles strolling into the room;
not any more, and the quick smoothing of the hair
was purely reflex.

'Hello, Kelly.' Linsday forced a hurried smile to
her lips as she opened the door to the girl from the
room next door.

Kelly Jordan bounded in, instantly filling the
small space with vitality. Probably the most exotic
woman Lindsay had ever come across, Kelly was
just on six feet tall, with a mass of jet-black hair, a
gorgeous face with eyes like saucers, and a smile
that would no doubt be beaming from every
magazine cover and billboard in London once the

modelling agencies got a chance to get her on to their books.

'Oh, good, you've got your coat on. Ready, then . . .?' Kelly flicked an eye over her, then broke into a peal of laughter as Linsday threw a surprised glance down at her coat as if she didn't quite know how she came to have it on. 'Yes, you have got it on,' Kelly assured her, trilling out another laugh as she met Lindsay's frown of puzzlement. 'What's the matter? Have you forgotten we were going shopping for a new outfit for me—for my round of the agencies next week—remember?

Lindsay's face cleared. 'Yes, of course. I hadn't really forgotten,' she smiled apologetically. 'I just got distracted by something. Sorry.'

'Are you OK?' Kelly's voice sharpened. 'You look a little . . .'

'I'm fine,' Lindsay cut in, quickly. 'A bit headachey, that's all. I didn't sleep very well last night.' That was putting it mildly. She'd spent a wretched night after Mr Barlow's revelations had sent her dreams of working for Ruytons up in smoke, and she hadn't managed to get over the searing disappointment of that, nor the churning anger towards Charles for having played her for an idiot, before Maggie's telegram turned up with its implied demand for instant action.

Kelly's deep brown eyes stayed fixedly on Lindsay's face. 'You do look pale,' she nodded after a long, assessing pause. 'I mean your tan looks lighter,' she amended with a little laugh. 'It's a fabulous tan. A tan like that in February—wow!'

Kelly breathed innocent envy.

'It's sizzling hot this time of year where I come from,' Lindsay reminded her—for the umpteenth time, since Kelly's comments on her tan had turned into a daily event, like the weather bulletin. 'And save your envy, it won't last much longer,' she added with a smile. 'Listen, Kelly, about the shopping trip . . . you won't mind if I don't come with you this afternoon, will you? There's something I need to attend to, and . . .'

'Heavens, no, of course I won't mind, only . . .' Kelly hesitated, looking faintly embarrassed. 'Honestly, Lindsay, please don't think I'm prying, but has something happened to upset you?' she asked diffidently.

It wasn't prying; Lindsay knew that. Kelly's concern was nothing if not genuine, and Linsday had a sudden urge to pour out the whole sorry story—about being taken in by Charles . . . the bounced cheque . . . her lost chance of working for Ruytons. It would have been lovely to wallow in a bit of sympathy and self-pity. Lindsay resisted the urge. 'Maree from reception brought up a telegram for me,' she said reluctantly, 'and . . .'

'Not bad news . . .? Your mother . . .?'

'She's fine,' Lindsay hurriedly checked Kelly's burst of anxiety. 'It was about a business matter—nothing very important,' she lied briskly, 'only I do need to see to it this afternoon, which is why I can't come shopping.'

'Oh, forget that.' Kelly swept a long hand through the air and almost hit a wall. 'And

anyway, I may not find anything I like. The clothes
are so boring this season, aren't they? And I do so
want to make an impression. It's important—
trying for the big-time, you know?'

Lindsay knew all about the desperate need to
succeed in your chosen field . . . wanting to be the
best; it was something they had in common and
which had drawn them into instant friendship
when they had found themselves neighbours. 'An
impression?' Lindsay grinned suddenly. 'Kelly,
darling, you'd make an impression in sackcloth
and ashes, and you know it. You look stunning as
you are.' Kelly was wearing an enormous black
cape over tight black jeans tucked into
preposterously high black highwayman's boots.
Anyone else would have looked absurd. Kelly
looked wonderful, and beside her Linsday felt
almost dowagerlike in the classic navy coat over
classic navy wool skirt and cream roll-neck
sweater.

'Do I really? Ta. You don't look bad yourself,'
Kelly grinned back, pleased and reassured,
amazing Linsday yet again that someone so
gorgeous could be so innocent of vanity and need
so much reassurance. 'You really are all right? OK,
OK, sorry. I know I'm nagging—comes from being
the eldest of a tribe of six,' Kelly laughed.
'Speaking of whom, I don't suppose you'd like to
come home with me to Dorset this weekend and
meet them . . .?' she asked, shyly. 'They'd love to
meet you.'

Lindsay was touched. 'I'd love to, Kelly, truly I

would, only not this weekend. Can we make it another time?' After she'd sorted out the opal business and could relax again was what Lindsay meant, but she couldn't explain that to her friend.

'Sure, whenever you like,' Kelly assured her cheerfully. 'Anyway, I'd better get moving . . .' She turned from the door. 'I won't be in until late tonight, and I'm leaving first thing in the morning, so I won't see you until Monday. Have a lovely weekend, whatever you're planning to do, won't you?' With a wave of the hand, Kelly swirled herself out of the room, and Lindsay heard her quick clatter down the first of the four flights of thin, worn carpet leading to the ground floor.

The room felt somehow colder, barer, without the warmth of Kelly's vibrant personality. Lindsay shivered and glanced at her watch: two-thirty. She could be at Ruytons by three. Should she telephone first . . .? And be put off by some smooth secretary? she answered herself with a grim laugh. No way. Hugh Rydon was not going to get the chance to refuse to see her. Lindsay was prepared to sit outside his office door for the rest of the afternoon if necessary, and if he genuinely wasn't in, she'd be back—again, and again, until he did see her, otherwise . . . The alternative made Lindsay feel nauseous. Police . . . solicitors . . . possibly a court case. It wouldn't come to that—couldn't, she assured herself. Ruytons wouldn't want a scandal on their hands any more than she did. They would locate Charles in Paris, or wherever he was, and either return the pendant to her or pay for it—Ruytons or cousin Hugh, Lindsay wasn't fussy.

The supercilious-looking saleswoman recognised her instantly, Lindsay could tell that from the glint of interest in the staring-through eyes as she approached, but otherwise the woman acted as if she had never clapped eyes on Lindsay before.

'I want to see Mr Rydon. Mr Hugh Rydon,' Lindsay emphasised coldly, hoping she wouldn't blush under the unwavering stare trained on her. She had spoken to this same woman twice this week, only it was Charles she had been enquiring about then, and now the sudden switch of Rydons must have had the saleswoman agog with curiosity behind the façade of polite indifference.

'You'll have to speak to the Gallery manager about that,' came the chilly, predictable reply.

'Yes, quite. Would you kindly get him for me?' Lindsay requested briskly.

She waited in the Gallery, not bothering to wander about as she had the last time, not even bothering to glance at the superb pieces in their beautiful display cabinets. They could all have been lumps of rock for all the interest they held for her now. The magic had gone from them—from Ruytons, too; it was just another jeweller.

The mirrored backing of the cabinet in front of her reflected a tall, stony-faced young woman, and then, as her consciousness focused on what her eyes were seeing, Lindsay realised that she was staring at herself and was quite shocked. How grim she looked, anger and nerves setting her face into a rigid mask, unnaturally brown between the sun-streaked blonde of the tightly drawn-back hair and the cream of the high-necked sweater showing above the collar of the coat. And, even from a distance, her deep blue eyes had a glazed, opaque look about them—lapis lazuli, the sapphire spark gone from them. Lindsay turned away and saw Mr Barlow coming towards her, his face pleasantly bland, everything else about him uneasy.

'I need to see Mr Hugh Rydon,' she began immediately, skipping the mandatory greeting, and something about her voice or the way she looked—possibly both, transmitted the unspoken message that she wasn't going to leave until she had seen him.

'Yes . . . well . . . I'll see what I can do. Miss Warren, isn't it?' The professional memory that must have charmed countless clients resurrected her name from their brief meeting the previous day. Lindsay gave a mechanical smile of acknowledgement.

She hadn't expected it to be easy, nor so quick, and stood about again while Mr Barlow went away to telephone someone, returning to say that Mrs Buchanan, Mr Rydon's deputy, would see her, and escorting her himself to the office of an extremely elegant middle-aged woman who suggested she might be of assistance, and was visibly miffed when Lindsay told her flatly that she might not, and that it was Mr Hugh Rydon she needed to see—in person on a private matter.

Another telephone call—to Hugh Rydon's

secretary this time by the sound of it, and, also from the sound of it, it seemed the secretary was offering to make an appointment.

'No appointment,' Lindsay cut through the start of Mrs Buchanan's reply. 'I want to see him today. Now.'

'Thank you, Sarah. I'll bring Miss Warren in to you.' Mrs Buchanan's faintly slackening jawline tightened noticeably as she put down the telephone. 'If you'll come with me, Miss Warren,' she invited through her teeth.

Only a belligerent anger and the knowledge that she had right on her side kept Lindsay from spinning on her heel and running out of the place in the face of such ice-polite intimidation. Her own jaw clamped achingly, she followed Mrs Buchanan out of the office, along a corridor, and up a flight of luxuriously carpeted stairs to what could only have been the inner sanctum. Hugh Rydon's waiting-room was a large L-shape and had an air of a private sitting-room about it: comfortable chairs, glowing rugs, landscapes on the walls.

His secretary was younger than Mrs Buchanan, but just as elegant. Perhaps you had to pass an elegance test to get a job here, Lindsay thought sourly as the cool green eyes assessed her impassively.

'I understand you wish to see Mr Rydon.' The voice wasn't warm either, carrying that ultra-politeness people use when they want to be very rude. 'I'm afraid Mr Rydon is in conference, but if you would care to tell me what it is you wish to discuss with him I could make an appointment for you.'

Lindsay hadn't come so far to be put off outside Hugh Rydon's door by an elegant brick wall of a secretary. 'I'll wait. As long as necessary,' she added, with ominous pleasantness, and, turning her back on the glare that brought a sudden life to the secretary's impassive face, she went over to the nearest chair and sat down, nonchalantly, she thought, but didn't really care. The anger was churning around in the pit of her stomach as she locked eyes with the secretary in a prolonged stare.

In the end, it was the secretary who dropped her eyes, spun on her heel and flounced to a door near the corner of the 'L' of the room, giving it one short rap before opening it with a sort of restrained fling, and closing it behind herself with a little slam.

Lindsay studied the face of an exquisite French antique clock on the small, highly polished table beside her. One and a half minutes ticked by.

'Mr Rydon will see you now,' the secretary told her, frigidly, emerging from the office and taking a few steps towards Lindsay, presumably so she wouldn't have to shout from the doorway.

So much for Hugh Rydon being 'in conference'.

'Thank you,' Lindsay said tightly, walking past the woman without a glance.

'Miss Warren,' she was announced, grudgingly, and then the door shut behind her.

The man seated at the desk at the far end of the room didn't look up. Disconcerted, Lindsay stared at the top of the dark head, then slid her eyes down to the tanned, well-shaped hand as it quickly attached a signature to a letter in the folder in front of him. She expected him to look up then, murmur an apology or something, but he didn't; he moved the folder aside, picked up another from the small, neat pile to his side and, opening it, began scanning a document.

Lindsay watched with a kind of angry fascination. There were a lot of ways of putting people in their place, and ignoring them was as good a way as any of making someone feel an inch tall. Hugh Rydon carried on his 'I'm terribly busy' act of calculated rudeness and Lindsay remained standing by the door, her face hot, mouth dry, nerves momentarily shot to pieces and feeling like a schoolgirl sent into the headmaster's office. Then the mass of anger inside her surged to the surface, and she was across the room and in front of the desk in a couple of fury-propelled strides.

'And good afternoon to you, Mr Rydon,' she enunciated precisely in a parody of politeness, the dripping sarcasm losing a lot of its impact because her voice shook so dreadfully.

The black head came up, slowly, and there wasn't a hint of discomfort in the hard eyes that ranged over her in a very deliberate, very unhurried appraisal which Lindsay felt missed nothing but her burgundy-coloured boots below the barrier of the desk.

She met the Arctic-grey eyes with a defiant lift of the chin as they returned to her face in a stare that

was all the more arrogant for seeming to look right
through her.

Hugh Rydon didn't apologise for having
continued his correspondence without acknow-
ledging her; he didn't stand up in a belated
greeting, didn't invite her to be seated, and if she
thought her taunt would embarrass this man into
courtesy, she was very mistaken. Lindsay felt really
unnerved as she stared back at him, trying hard not
to flinch.

'Yes, Miss Warren . . .? There was a faint echo
of Charles' voice under the barely restrained snap
of impatience, but with more timbre in it, and,
while there was also a look of Charles about the
strong, rather prominent nose, there the family
resemblance came to an abrupt halt, because
however much of a rogue Charles had been, at least
he'd been personable, had charm, if too much of
it; his cousin obviously hadn't a skerrick, and was
about as personable as a rock. What he did have,
though, was an air of something solid, substantial
about him that Charles had never had.
Monumental arrogance aside, Hugh Rydon
radiated an authority and self-assurance that put
Charles' easygoing confidence into head-prefect
class. Lindsay had never disliked anyone so
instinctively, so thoroughly.

'Yes, Miss Warren . . .?' Hugh Rydon repeated
in a voice that could have frosted glass. Capping
his slim, gold pen, he set it down on top of the
document in the open folder, then, leaning slightly
back in his chair, studied her flushed face with no

expression except a sort of bored blandness over the hard-edged, handsome features. Yet the eyes did have something new in them—something that hadn't been there at the first lift of the head . . . a glimmer of interest, or curiosity, Lindsay thought.

'I . . . I wanted to see Charles—your cousin . . . Charles Rydon. I . . . he . . .' Lindsay trailed off, half reduced to incoherence by her nerves and her mouth so dry that she had to swallow once or twice and run the tip of her tongue over her parched lips, her every nervous move watched with sardonic interest from under one black, raised brow as Hugh Rydon waited for her to go on. 'I wanted to see Charles,' Lindsay began again.

The upward tilt of the corner of his mouth was a borderline sneer. 'I think we can take that as read, Miss Warren, since I've already gathered as much from your forays into this establishment during the past week,' he told her drily, 'not to mention the telephone enquiries you so felt the need to make . . . five in all, wasn't it, or have I missed hearing about more?'

Lindsay felt her face burning.

'However,' Hugh Rydon continued, the curve of malice disappearing as his lips set into a thin, hard line, and his voice hardening, 'as *you* surely must have gathered by now, my cousin is not available—and I use the word advisedly. I believe you were told Charles is in Paris—with his wife, and I assure you the information is correct on both counts, if it's verification from me that has brought you so determinedly into this office.' He sat back and watched her face as the impact of what he'd said hit home—not the information itself, because he hadn't told her anything new, but his appalling implied assumption that she was a cast-off girlfriend who wouldn't believe Charles was married, or that she'd been cast off and had been coming in to Ruytons to pester her erstwhile lover.

It wasn't true, any of it, but all the same Lindsay wanted the floor to open and swallow her . . . anything to get out of sight of this disdainful, arrogant man who had apparently been kept informed of her every contact with Ruytons and jumped to his own—wrong—conclusions, and who very obviously considered her beneath even the pretence of politeness. Lindsay felt weak with the rush of mortification. She took a deep breath. 'I know your cousin is in Paris. With his wife,' she said with as much dignity as she could muster, and it was an effort to keep the shake out of her voice. 'And I'm not here for any verification from you, Mr Rydon.' Lindsay flicked a glance down at his open folder. 'I know you're a very busy man, but I had to insist on seeing you because . . . because Charles owes me money,' she finished in a rush, and could not have put it more bluntly if she'd tried . . . could not have felt more humiliated—cheap—having it come out like that. It would have felt less dreadful saying, 'Your cousin is a conman—a thief.' Yet somehow she hadn't been able to say that.

It was disconcerting to see no surprise when the

normal reaction would surely have been to show some. There was just a slight tensing of the jaw, and that seemed to be the extent of Hugh Rydon's reaction to her bald statement, until Lindsay saw the distate—or was it straight-out contempt—in the steely grey eyes? And then she didn't know where to look.

'I see,' he said icily, after a very long pause. 'And in Charles' absence, you've come to me to . . . collect? Is that it, Miss Warren?'

It was. And yet Lindsay had the uneasy sense that it wasn't. Her small, jerky nod of assent was at variance with her frown of puzzlement. She watched, perplexed, as he slipped a hand into the inside of the superbly, expensively cut dark jacket and drew out a slim, leather folder. The cheque-book came out in silence, and the silence continued as Hugh Rydon picked up the gold pen and uncapped it.

'How much, Miss Warren?' he asked, tonelessly, without interest, it seemed, and without looking at her. His eyes were lowered to the cheque-book on the desk, hand poised over it.

Lindsay's heart gave a thump. This was all wrong . . . no surprise; no questions; no demand for explanation. 'Twenty thousand pounds,' she answered, evenly, and was ready to meet the disbelieving eyes as they lifted suddenly to her, the black brows shooting up with the first sign of surprise Hugh Rydon had shown since she had walked into the room.

'Will you repeat that, please?' he requested

through compressed lips in a voice that was like slivers of ice, and with such open, searing contempt in his eyes that Lindsay was quite shocked.

Her hands began to shake uncontrollably at her sides and she rammed them into her coat pockets, her right hand touching Maggie's scrunched-up telegram and then closing around it tightly. The feel of the small ball of crumpled paper made an amazing, reassuring difference—it was the remainder she needed that she had a very good reason to be here confronting the head of Ruytons, and she wasn't going to let herself be intimidated by him a moment longer. His personal opinion of her be damned, Lindsay thought, with a welcome rush of the hot anger that had temporarily been shocked out of her.

Her eyes flashed dangerously. 'Oh, I think you heard me, Mr Rydon,' she tossed back with a hard, brittle brightness that seemed to take Hugh Rydon by surprise. 'But yes, certainly, I will repeat it for you. Your cousin, Charles Rydon, owes me twenty thousand pounds,' she repeated slowly and with mock preciseness. 'Is that clear enough for you? Oh, and I'd prefer a Ruytons company cheque if it's all the same to you. I've found that personal cheques have rather an unfortunate tendency to bounce.' Lindsay twisted out a snaky smile.

Tit for tat. Two could play at scoring cheap points, and she felt a self-congratulatory flare of triumph that she was getting her own back on the impossibly rude man. It was not her imagination: a dark, angry red was surging slowly up Hugh

Rydon's throat above the crisp whiteness of his collar, and meandering up into his granite-set face.

Eyes narrowed to darkly lashed slits, he glared at her across the barrier of the desk, and Lindsay glared back defiantly. And then, unaccountably, and to Lindsay's incredulous fury, the angry eyes left her face and slid down her body to come to a long, suggestive halt around her abdomen.

'Are you pregant, Miss Warren?' Hugh Rydon asked coolly, flicking his eyes suddenly back to her rigid face.

CHAPTER TWO

LINDSAY felt quite faint as the blood rushed from her face in a violent sweep. She opened her mouth and shut it again, bringing her teeth together with an audible snap, and staring in stunned disbelief at the preposterous man behind the desk who sat looking at her, a tiny flicker of a smile at the corner of his mouth as he savoured her amazement—and the point he'd scored.

Lindsay tried out her voice at last. 'Am I . . . Am I what . . .?' she demanded, hardly able to get the harsh, breathy words out for fury. 'How dare you? How dare you ask me such a thing . . .?' she blazed at him, and thought she would have an apoplectic fit as she saw her rage dance off him without ruffling a line of the smug expression.

Hugh Rydon gazed back, unperturbed, then gave an abrupt bark of a laugh. 'You'll have to forgive my impertinence, Miss Warren,' he said with a fatuously smooth regret that made mockery of his apology. 'I don't normally ask such personal questions of ladies, and from your performance of outraged virtue I'll take it the answer is in the negative.' The voice took on a sudden, nastily hard edge. 'That being the case, may I suggest you reconsider the amount you're inviting me to fork

28

out as compensation for the inconvenience and out-of-pocket expenses you've incurred in following my cousin to London—I assume in the expectation of continuing the affair which must have begun during Charles's brief visit to Sydney?'

Lindsay felt her eyes jerk half-way up into her forehead, and her jaw slacken as it dropped probably four inches.

'I quite understand your chagrin at finding yourself a victim of a straying married man,' Hugh Rydon went on, with what perhaps he thought was an understanding smile, but which was, in fact, a grimace of distaste. 'But you're a very attractive woman, Miss Warren, as you yourself must know, and I'm sure you'll soon find someone to help you recover from your disappointment.' He sounded ludicrously like a doctor dispensing soothing advice, except that every amazing word he was saying was making Lindsay feel sick. Only incredulous, appalled fascination kept her rooted in front of the desk, and she was conscious of a mad curiosity as to what he could possibly come out with next.

'However,' the soothing flow of words continued, 'I accept that you would feel better a whole lot sooner with some immediate and tangible compensation. Shall we say, two thousand pounds? That, I think, should cover your air fare to England and out-of-pocket expenses,' he suggested, quite pleasantly, but only the voice carried that spurious pleasantness; his eyes, as Lindsay stared into them a little wildly, scorched her with their contempt. Then all pretence of

pleasantness vanished. 'I rather think expectations
of anything higher could be construed as
blackmail, don't you, Miss Warren?' There was an
unmistakable warning in the voice.

Lindsay thought she'd already heard everything,
but Hugh Rydon's inventiveness really floored her.
She couldn't believe her ears. 'Blackmail?' she
mouthed weakly.

'Blackmail, Miss Warren. And frankly, I would
have thought you'd have had more pride than to
stoop to attempt it.'

The lecturing, consorious note was the last
straw. Lindsay saw red. 'That's quite enough, Mr
Rydon,' she hissed, lunging across the desk at him
and startling him into hurriedly backing deeper
into his chair. Lindsay straightened up with a shrill
laugh that grated on her own ears. 'And since we're
being so frank about each other, let me tell you
that you are the most arrogant, the most nasty-
minded man I have ever met. You . . . you're
unspeakable . . .!' Words really and truly failed
her. Frustrated, Lindsay yanked her hand out of
her pocket and might have actually hit him, but,
finding she was still clutching the scrunched-up
telegram, let fly at Hugh Rydon's head with it. If
she'd had a rock in her hand, it probably would
have gone in the same direction.

She didn't wait to see it hit its target; she spun
round and made a dash for the door.

'Miss Warren . . . Lindsay . . . Wait!' Hugh
Rydon called out in angry surprise as Lindsay flung
herself out of the room.

She had no recollection of finding her way out of the building. One moment she was hurling her missile at Hugh Rydon, the next she was charging out of the Gallery into that unbelievably early darkness which had so astounded her on her first day in London.

The rain was pelting down as she dashed out from under the covers of Ruytons' burgundy and navy awning and ran along the footpath, jostling and being jostled by the stream of passers-by hurrying through the downpour.

Blackmail. Hugh Rydon had virtually accused her of attempting to blackmail him . . . blackmail Charles. About a supposed affair . . .? Just what sort of woman did he think she was . . .? Immoral . . . vindictive . . . money-grubbing—and that was just for starters. She had never been so insulted in her life. Her mind a whirl of mortification and rage, Lindsay ran towards the intersection, blinking against the rain and the distorted glare of car and streetlights swimming fuzzily in front of her eyes.

'Look out!'

The shout registered above the grind of the traffic, the rain, and the swish of tyres on the wet road as Lindsay darted off the kerb. Half turning towards the voice behind her, she felt a grab at her arm, then felt herself falling. Her last conscious thought before everything went black was that her head hurt, and then, when the blackness cleared, her head was still hurting.

Lindsay lay with her eyes closed, knowing that if

she tried to open them her head would hurt more. She mumbled something indistinct, a petulant protest directed at no one in particular, and let her mind drift away again.

'Lindsay . . .'

The voice above her head sounded familiar, 'Charles . . .' she murmured sleepily, ungluing her eyelids a fraction and looking up into Hugh Rydon's grey eyes.

'Hugh,' he corrected her, stiffly.

'Go away,' Lindsay mumbled, closing her eyes, and the next time she opened them there was nobody there.

She must have dreamt Hugh Rydon had been standing at her bedside. Without turning her head, Lindsay curved her eyes around the room—a hospital room. She wasn't surprised, because somewhere along the line, some part of her brain had taken in the sounds and smells and identified them with a hospital, but what she couldn't work out—and it seemed too much trouble to try—was how she came to be in one.

'Hello, dear, you're awake. That's a good girl. You've been sleeping far too much. Doctor doesn't like it.'

What was it about being a patient that made nurses treat you like a retarded six-year-old? This one looked only a couple of years older than herself. Lindsay glowered in silence as firm, cool fingers lifted her hand up, then snapped around her wrist to take her pulse.

'What am I doing here?' she asked as the nurse

went to the end of the bed to jot something on to the bedchart.

The nurse gave a laugh. 'Getting over a near encounter with a big bus.'

Lindsay frowned. Bus . . .? She couldn't remember any bus, but then, all at once, she remembered the voice calling out 'look out' and the snatch at her arm . . . falling . . . Damn, she thought, of all the stupid things to do. And then she remembered a whole lot more . . . Hugh Rydon . . . blackmail, and groaned aloud.

'Head hurting?' The nurses's eyes sharpened.

Lindsay tried to shake her head and found her neck didn't want to, and when she tried to lift her hand up to investigate she also found her arm and shoulder hurt abominably. 'What's the matter with me?' she demanded bad-temperedly.

'Just a few bumps and bruises where you made contact with a hard kerb,' the nurse told her unsympathetically. 'A small cut on your right temple—that's why the plaster is there, so don't go touching it,' she ordered as Lindsay made a tentative gesture with her hand.

'Is that all?' Lindsay muttered. It seemed very little to land her in a hospital.

'Not enough for you?' the nurse grinned. 'Add concussion to the list if it makes you happier, and consider yourself very lucky someone pulled you out of the way of that bus, or you wouldn't be considering anything at all.'

'Oh,' Lindsay said absently, frowning at the darkness outside the window. It had been dark

when she'd stormed out of Ruytons. Was it only
hours ago? 'What day is it?' she asked suddenly,
suspecting it might already be Saturday.

'Sunday. Six o'clock. Dinner will be coming
around soon.'

'Sunday?' Lindsay yelped in surprise. 'How
much longer do I need to stay? I'm all right, aren't
I? You're not keeping anything back from me?'
she asked suspiciously, wriggling her toes
frantically under the bedclothes and relieved to
find movement in them.

'Why on earth should we? You're fine,' the
nurse assured her. 'You'll even be discharged
tomorrow after the doctor has seen you again, so
why don't you relax now and think about your
lovely friend?'

Friend? Kelly? How on earth did Kelly find out
she was in here?

'And you haven't even looked at your beautiful
flowers yet, nor opened the envelope.'

Lindsay had seen the flowers, and yet not seen
them . . . not taken them in. She looked at them
now. Bright golden daffodils, wonderfully
coloured tulips—hothouse and very expensive.
Kelly? She frowned at the nurse. 'But how did
Kelly know?'

'Kelly? Is that his name?'

'His . . .? Who . . .?'

The nurse looked at her curiously. 'The friend
who came in after you were admitted—you know,
the one who came to see you this afternoon and
brought the flowers. Oh, that's right, you were

asleep and he didn't want to disturb you, but he said he'd come tomorrow to take you home. Lucky girl,' the young nurse grinned enviously. 'I'd probably try throwing myself under a bus too, to have him come and visit me.'

'I did not throw myself under a bus,' Lindsay snapped, and looked sullenly about the room. 'And I suppose my "friend" organised this private room? It is a private room, I suppose?' It couldn't be anything but, and left her shabby hotel room for dead.

'Yes, it is a private room. You were moved into here straight from Casualty, and you'd better talk to your friend about it if you don't like it, because yes, he was the one who arranged it.;'

Oh, she'd be speaking to him all right—through a hard-nosed solicitor just as soon as she got out of here, Lindsay promised herself vehemently—and after the nurse had gone she picked up the envelope propped against the vase of flowers and looked at it in distaste. 'Lindsay Warren' was written across it in a firm, distinctive hand, and Lindsay had a vision of that strong, brown hand poised over the cheque-book, gold pen at the ready. Was the cheque in the envelope? Two thousand pounds, he had offered—air fares and expenses, with a bit extra thrown in to cover the odd private room in hospital, no doubt, she thought acidly, and slowly and deliberately tore the envelope in half, then in half again, and tossed the four pieces on to the top of the bedside table beside the vase.

'Like that, is it?' The nursed eyed the pieces of

torn envelope curiously when she came back after dinner.

'Like what?' muttered Lindsay before a thermometer was popped into her mouth.

The nurse grinned slyly as she took Lindsay's pulse. 'You're allowed to get up and go to the bathroom yourself now when you want,' she said, coming over all brisk as she removed the thermometer and went to make her jottings on the bedchart.

'What a treat. Goody, goody,' Lindsay returned tartly.

'You really must be feeling better to be snapping at me like that,' the nurse chuckled, disappearing out the door and leaving it open behind her.

Lindsay glowered at the empty doorway and then at the flowers again, and later, at herself in the bathroom—her own private bathroom, compliments of Hugh Rydon. She examined the bruising, gingerly running her hand down the side of her face, and then feeling the large bump on the side of her head. She looked a sight and the unflattering hospital gown didn't make her look any better. Irrationally, she suddenly thought of Hugh Rydon's having seen her like that and was furious. How dared he come to see her after his monstrous performance in his office? And how did he know she'd been in an accident, anyway?

That was something she would have to live without knowing, Lindsay decided, because she had no intention of being around to ask him when—if—he turned up the next day. She planned on leaving very early in the morning—but hadn't allowed for hospital routine, and nearly went out of her mind with frustration when she was still sitting about in her nightgown at eleven o'clock, forced to wait for the doctor's round before being allowed to get dressed and check out.

And when he finally did come, it took all of two minutes to inspect her cut, tell her to take it easy, and that she was free to go. All that waiting for nothing. Lindsay was livid. She dressed hurriedly, and was in the bathroom, trying to smooth as much hair as she could over the side of her face, when she heard someone calling out, and emerged from the bathroom to find a nurse she hadn't seen before shepherding Hugh Rydon into the room.

'Your friend is here to take you home.' The nurse flashed them both a smile and left them to stare at each other in dead silence.

She hadn't seen Hugh Rydon on his feet—apart from the hazy recollection of a tall figure by her bed. Lindsay flicked a rapid eye over him—much as he had done when he'd first looked her over . . . taller than she would have supposed, a hard leanness about him, and looking the epitome of a very successful businessman in the mandatory dark suit. Impressive—attractive, too, Lindsay had to admit, and that somehow made her angrier with him.

'What the hell do you think you're doing here?' she demanded, hostile.

The smile was tentative. A very nice smile, and this was the first time she had seen it. 'How do

you feel? You're looking much better.' He ignored
her question and, it seemed to Lindsay, was
keeping his eyes off her bruising and plaster with
careful tact.

Her hand shot up automatically to bring more
hair over that side of her face—an instinctive,
feminine response to an attractive man, and
Lindsay could have kicked herself for it. She
dropped her hand angrily.

'I see you've read my note,' Hugh smiled wryly,
flicking a nod at the torn piece of envelope still
lying on the bedside table.

Lindsay gave a grunt of derision. 'You flatter
yourself, Mr Rydon. And you still haven't
answered my question. I asked what you're doing
here.'

He shrugged lightly. 'I came to take you home. I
did ask the nurse to tell you yesterday when I
called,' he added, defensively.

'I'll take myself home, thank you, Mr Rydon,'
Lindsay told him frigidly. 'And I don't know how
you managed to ferret me out in here, but let me
tell you, your touching spate of concern—this
private room . . . those,' she waved a hand towards
the flowers, 'won't wash with me. I'll be seeing a
solicitor today. Your cousin stole a valuable opal
from me—my mother—and I intend kicking up the
biggest stink Ruytons has ever had on its hands if I
don't get it back. So, Mr Rydon,' Lindsay smiled
sneeringly, 'I suggest you go back to your office
and either hunt up your cousin and the opal, or get
on to your own solicitor, because you're going to

need one.' Then her shaky self-control deserted her and her voice shook with anger. 'And if you dare, ever again, speak to me as you did the other day, I . . .' Lindsay broke off, unable to think of a threat she could possibly carry out. 'Oh, go away,' she muttered, and thought he was leaving when he turned to the door, but he only closed it, then stood with his back against it, looking at her.

'We're not going anywhere until you've heard me out,' Hugh said crisply. 'First of all, I did not "ferret" you out as you so colourfully put it. The hospital telephoned Ruytons on Friday after your . . . accident.' His lips twisted faintly as he gave the last word a strange emphasis that made Lindsay frown. 'It seems the only clue they had as to who you might be was Ruytons' address and phone number in your handbag, and they thought perhaps you were one of our employees, which is why they telephoned us.'

It was a perfectly reasonable explanation, and Lindsay had no option but to accept it.

'However,' Hugh's voice softened, 'under other circumstances, I might have had to do a bit of "ferreting" to find you—to apologise for my behaviour towards you at our meeting. After I'd spoken to Charles in Paris, I realised I'd made a regrettable mistake.' Hugh smiled apologetically.

A regrettable mistake? Lindsay's eyes blazed. 'How big of you,' she hissed scornfully, 'but if you think . . .'

'And if you'd read my note before shredding it,' he cut her off sharply, 'you would have had the explanation for my rather curious assumptions about you. There is an explanation, strange as it may seem to you, but I shan't bore you with it right now. I will say, though, that I'm sorry about my mistake. Very sorry. I mean that, Lindsay.' Hugh looked at her, one heavy, dark eyebrow raised questioningly as he waited—for her 'Oh, that's all right, forget it'? 'And as for your opal,' he went on when Lindsay couldn't find words for her fury, 'I assure you it's quite safe, and Charles had no intention of stealing it. So that, at least, is one less sin against him.' He smiled drily into Lindsay's glare. 'The mix-up about the cheque was unfortunate, but can easily be recified.'

Lindsay stared at him wonderingly. What sort of man could virtually accuse someone of blackmail—and lord only knew what else—then calmly turn around and dismiss it with a careless 'made a mistake, sorry'? She had never come across such arrogance in her life. 'I want that opal back,' she ground through her teeth.

Hugh shrugged. 'If that's what you want.'

'Yes, that is what I want—and for you to get out of here. I never want to set eyes on you or your double-crossing cousin again.' Lindsay snatched up her coat from the bed and then winced with the effort of raising her arm to ram it into the sleeve. 'Leave me alone,' she barked, as Hugh came over and tried to help her into it.

The door swung open. 'Hello, are you still here? I trust I'm not intruding?' The nurse smiled coyly—mainly at Hugh.

Lindsay pulled away from him, flushing
furiously as she realised the woman thought she'd
interrupted an embrace. She struggled, unaided,
into her coat and grabbed her handbag off the bed.

'I think we're ready to leave now.' Hugh smiled
at the nurse and put a very firm hand under
Lindsay's elbow.

'Well, take good care of her and don't let her
walk under another bus,' the nurse instructed
Hugh facetiously, and was high-handedly brisk to
Lindsay herself. 'Please remember what the doctor
said, Miss Warren—plenty of bed-rest for the next
day or two and then take things very slowly.'

'Certainly, Nurse. Thank you,' Hugh had the
cheek to answer for her as he led her out of the
room under the nurse's approving eye.

He had his limousine waiting . . . double-parked
outside the hospital's main entrance; the driver
leapt out to open the door when he spotted them
coming down the steps, Hugh's hand still at her
elbow. Lindsay climbed into the back seat in sullen
silence, and, while she wouldn't have admitted it to
save her life, was glad of the lift. Just getting to the
car had taken more out of her than she'd have
believed; two buses home would have been
unbearable—and buses it would have been,
because she didn't have the fare for such a long
ride in a cab.

Grudgingly, she muttered the address of the
hotel when Hugh got in beside her, then, clamping
her mouth shut, leant back against the head-rest,
her eyes firmly closed to discourage further

communication—and to give herself time to get a
grip on herself. Every nerve seemed to have
become maddeningly aware of the man at her side
during their long, silent walk out of the hospital.
She felt tense, and stupidly nervous of him, and
vaguely afraid that, given half the chance, Hugh
Rydon would have her believing it was perfectly
acceptable that he should insult her one day and be
forgiven at the drop of a hat three days later
because he smiled charmingly and said, 'Sorry.'
Lindsay kept her eyes determinedly closed.

'I think we're here. Is this it?' Hugh touched her
hand lightly, waking her from the doze she had
unintentionally drifted into.

Lindsay yanked her hand out from under his and
saw the shabby, bulky Victorian façade of the
hotel, with its fat, peeling columns at the top of the
steps which led from the footpath to the entrance.
'Yes. Thank you for the lift, Mr Rydon. Please see
to the return of the opal,' she said with stiff
formality, and, releasing the door catch, had
swung the door open before the driver had a
chance to get to it. 'Thank you,' she muttered at
him as she shot past, and was already half-way up
the steps before Hugh caught up with her, taking
hold of her arm and pulling her to a stop.

'Take it easy, Lindsay. You shouldn't be dashing
like that.'

'Take your hand off me, and when I want your
medical opinion I'll ask for it,' Lindsay snapped at
him, jerking her arm out of his grasp and starting
up the steps again, but taking them much more

more slowly—not because she'd been ordered to, but because the first frantic pelt from the kerb had made her dizzy.

She ignored him as he followed her into the reception area.

'Lindsay . . . hi,' Maree called out from the desk. 'Been away? Good grief, what have you done to yourself?'

Lindsay ignored the question. 'Any messages?' she asked curtly.

Maree shook her head, no longer looking at Lindsay. The Hugh Rydons of the world were few and far between in this neck of the woods, and among the faded gentility of the shabby reception he looked as if he'd lost his way from another world—planet. Lindsay saw the brightening of the eyes, the flirtatiousness in the batty smile Maree was focusing on him, and winced.

She marched across the hall and stopped at the bottom of the staircase. 'Thank you again, Mr Rydon. There's no need for you to come any further.' She kept her voice down; Maree was out of sight, but not out of earshot. 'And if you would just see to the opal, we needn't bother each other again.'

'Don't be an idiot.' Hugh took her arm again. 'Come on, slowly, though. Or would you prefer I carry you?' He smiled threateningly, making no attempt to keep his voice down as she had done.

Lindsay gave in with a scowl and then tried to get rid of him again when they'd climbed the four breathtaking flights to her room, and might have saved what was left of her breath. 'Thank you, Mr Rydon . . .' she just got out before Hugh cut her off.

'For heaven's sake, Lindsay,' he snapped irritably, 'I know you're mad at me—and yes, with reason, but could you try climbing off that high horse and call me Hugh? And I'm coming in, invited or not, and I'm staying, like it or not, until we've talked this misunderstanding through. Now, come on, let's get inside.'

The room seemed smaller, shabbier than when she had left it, and was definitely colder. Hugh went straight over to the electric heater and switched it on.

'Keep your coat on for the moment,' he ordered, eyeing her with concern. 'And lie down on the bed for a while. I'll organise some tea.' He cast an eye around the room, managing not to show the distaste he must have felt. 'I don't suppose there's such a thing as room service?' he asked, not very hopefully.

Lindsay laughed gratingly. 'What do you think?' she retorted, remaining standing in the centre of the tiny room, although she would have loved to fling herself down on the bed and catch her breath after the climb. That would have made him think she was obeying him.

'I'll be back shortly,' Hugh said suddenly, and disappeared out of the door.

Startled, Lindsay stared after him, then gave a shrug which made her bruised shoulder yelp in protest. She rubbed it gingerly through the coat and went to stand at the window, where the same grey scene met her eyes—greyer and colder-looking than Friday, even, and she felt cold and grey to match. The aftermath of the accident, she told herself, because she should have been feeling at least relieved, if not ecstatic, knowing that she'd be getting the opal back by the end of the day. She trusted Hugh Rydon to see to that—the extent of her trust of him. Everything else about him had her bristling with suspicion.

Just why was he falling over himself being concerned and helpful? It didn't make any sense to her. The opal was not stolen, so she wouldn't be kicking up a fuss about it, nor darkening Ruytons' elegant Gallery again. So . . .? Making amends for having misjudged her . . .? Lindsay wasn't convinced. To someone of Hugh Rydon's arrogance, a curt apology sufficed, and he had already tossed that to her.

CHAPTER THREE

'YOU should be lying down,' Hugh reprimanded her from the doorway, and Lindsay turned to see him come in carrying a tray with a teapot and two cups set on it. 'The receptionist was very obliging,' he answered the unspoken question in her face.

Of course. 'I bet she was,' Lindsay muttered tartly, thinking what pushovers most women seemed to become when men like Hugh Rydon laid on the charm.

'Miaow . . .' Hugh flashed her a sudden, cheeky grin which had the effect of lighting up his face and making him look mischievously boyish.

It caught Lindsay by surprise and, unthinkingly, she laughed, genuinely amused.

'You shouldn't be standing about. The nurse said bed-rest, remember . . .?'

The amusement flicked off her face like a light. 'Don't order me about—and what the nurse said to me is none of your business. So, can the advice, unless you're planning a change of career and are about to turn nurse yourself.'

He thought that was funny. 'Can't see myself in the uniform, can you?' he chuckled, placing the tray down on the dressing-table sort of thing, which was the only flat surface in the room.

'Well, at least sit down and have a cup of tea, or all that charm of mine will have been wasted.' He grinned again, disarmingly, and against her better judgement Lindsay allowed herself to be disarmed—for the moment.

She sat down resignedly on the one chair in the room. 'Look, Mr Rydon——' she began, terribly reasonably.

'Hugh.'

'Hugh, then,' Lindsay gave in ungraciously. 'Well, Hugh,' she bit into the name testily, 'don't you think you're going a little overboard in making up for your despicable behaviour on Friday?' The flash of scowl was for her choice of adjective. Lindsay repeated the word deliberately. 'It was despicable and uncalled-for—however,' she raised her voice, running on quickly to pre-empt his interruption, 'you have apologised, and I . . . I accept your apology. And now, since you've promised to return my opal, let's call it quits. You can cut the mother-hen act, it's getting on my nerves, and frankly, you're not cut out for it.'

Hugh poured the tea, the muscles of his face tightening into that almost expressionless aloofness that had so intimidated her in his office. He handed her the cup in a silence full of a tension that hadn't been there a few moments ago. 'I owe you an explanation,' he said tightly, 'and you owe it to me to listen to it.'

'Owe . . .?' Lindsay flared with indignation. She put her cup back on to the tray with a clatter. 'Owe it to you . . .?'

Hugh turned away from her without picking up his own cup of tea. There wasn't any space in the room to pace about in; he stood irresolutely for a moment before moving to the door and leaning a shoulder against it as he studied her with something very like dislike, but which, oddly, Lindsay found easier to take than the impenetrable aloofness.

'Why didn't you tell me about that damned opal when you came bursting into my office on Friday, instead of letting me plough headlong into my assumptions about you?' Hugh demanded accusingly, and quite flabbergasted Lindsay with the utter unreasonableness of the attack.

'Now, hold it. Just hold it right there, *Mister* Rydon,' she hurled at him. 'You're the one who's supposed to be offering explanations, not me. And I didn't exactly get the opportunity to tell you anything, did I? So don't you dare start blaming me for your outrageous assumptions; they were all the work of your very own nasty little mind. And what was I supposed to be blackmailing you—Charles—about, anyway?' Lindsay added belligerently as her curiosity reared unexpectedly. 'You surely can't mean that just because Charles is married . . .? Good heavens, I believe you do,' she jeered into his angrily glittering eyes. 'You do realise which century we're living in, don't you?' Lindsay cackled, and suddenly stopped dead as it struck her that her crack was practically confirmation of his assumption that she and Charles had had an affair. And from Hugh's stony face, it was apparent that was how he took it. 'I . . .

we . . .' Lindsay began, and didn't know how to go on.

'Please don't explain. It's not my business,' Hugh said with the familiar ice in his voice. 'However . . .'

'No, damn it, it isn't!' Lindsay retorted, her cheeks red, furious with herself for caring one iota that this man believed her capable of hopping into bed with anyone after three weeks' acquaintanceship. Even if she had been madly in love with Charles she would never have done that, and she would never have embarked on an affair with any married man if her life depended on it. Who did Hugh Rydon think he was, to cast aspersions on her morals with his holier-than-thou distaste . . .?

'However, what I did feel was my business on Friday,' Hugh continued as if she hadn't burst out with her retort, 'was to keep my cousin's latest little fling from his wife, who happens to be my sister, and who also happens to be pregnant with their first child,' he added, smiling mirthlessly at Lindsay's shocked surprise at what an absolute rat Charles had been—was. 'And, strange as it may seem, the last thing Charles wants is to hurt his wife—or his marriage. All right,' he conceded testily as Lindsay's face showed her scepticism. 'I know that's hard to believe, but the man is an idiot, and I dare say my sister is even more of one for bothering with him. The trouble with Charles,' he continued, almost chattily, 'is that he can't seem to resist an attractive woman when he's away from

home, only his affairs have never meant anything
to him. Not flattering to you, but there you are
. . .' Hugh's eyes gleamed with malice. 'Charles
had always been like that.'

'A philanderer,' Lindsay put in coldly.

Hugh shrugged indifference. 'Yes, if you like.
Only some of his ladies tend to become more
involved than he bargains for, and there was one in
the not-so-distant past who was exceptionally put
out, and wasn't prepared to fade quietly from the
scene.'

'So you bought her off,' Lindsay grated out
scornfully.

Hugh shook his head. 'Charles settled the
matter. This time, however, since he was away and
you were so very persistent, and Ruytons looked
like being involved, I thought that . . .'

'Don't bother with the details. I know what you
thought and it makes me sick,' Lindsay burst out
heatedly.

'I said I was sorry,' Hugh muttered gruffly.

'Oh, and that makes everything all right, does
it?' Lindsay sprang from the chair and went
agitatedly to the window, staring out through an
unexpected blur of tears.

'No, it doesn't make everything all right,' Hugh
murmured softly behind her. Lindsay tensed and
brushed a surreptitious hand over her eyes. 'What
did he promise you?' he asked in a low, unemotioal
voice. 'I know he must have promised something to
bring you to the other side of the world,' Hugh
persisted as Lindsay stared deafly ahead. 'It can't

have been for love . . .' He sounded curiously
unsure, and underneath the unsureness Lindsay
detected an edge of anger; under different
circumstances she might have said jealousy, but
under these circumstances the notion was absurd,
because Hugh Rydon couldn't possibly have been
jealous of his cousin, even if she and Charles had
had a raging affair—which they hadn't. A light-
hearted romance, and if Charles hadn't been a
Rydon, there would not even have been that. God,
what a little opportunist she had been—
unconsciously, maybe, but it left a sour taste in
Lindsay's mouth.

'I was coming anyway,' she mumbled.

'But he did promise you something. He always
does. Charles is nothing if not predictable in his
affairs.'

It wasn't an affair, Lindsay wanted to shout; she
shook her head miserably. Why bother? Let him
think what he wanted. She could feel the warmth
of his arm against hers, and felt herself going rigid
with the tension of having him so near her. 'It was
a damned fool thing you did, you idiot,' Hugh
rasped harshly, and startled her into turning to face
him. He gave an angry laugh. 'Was it just a try-on?
To bring him running to your hospital bed?' he
asked, a bitter twist to his mouth; it took Lindsay a
good few moments to work out what he meant,
and then she had trouble believing it.

Hugh thought that she'd deliberately thrown
herself under a bus? Because of Charles? A little
laugh gurgled out of her throat, and then refused

to stop. Jaw clamped tight, Hugh watched as she struggled with the hysteria. 'I thought you would have had more sense. So what did he promise you?' he returned to the question abruptly, and unwittingly Lindsay muttered,

'A job.'

'At Ruytons?'

'Where else?' she shot back, her eyes flashing at his surprise and the implication that she wasn't good enough for Ruytons.

'Oh.' Hugh gave his chin a distracted rub. 'As a salesgirl . . . I see. That might still be possible—if you're still interested,' he offered, with a questioning smile that didn't last long in the face of Lindsay's glare.

'No, I am not interested,' she barked, professional hackles quivering, 'and I'll thank you not to patronise me, Mr Rydon. I'm a designer—a damned good one at that—and I wouldn't take a job with Ruytons if they were the last jewellery house left in the business.'

Hugh stepped back from her, astonished, a comprehension dawning in his eyes. 'That pendant . . . I didn't realise . . .'

'Lindsay!'

The voice startled them and they both swung their eyes to the door.

'Lindsay, helloo, it's me . . .'

Kelly. Lindsay pushed past Hugh and went to open the door.

'Lindsay!' Kelly shrieked, her eyes widening to about twice their enormous size. 'Your face . . .

you're hurt! What happened?'

'For heaven's sake, Kelly, I'm all right. Just a small accident,' Lindsay snapped. 'Do you want to come in?' she invited, ungraciously, as Kelly hovered at the door, her eyes already over Lindsay's shoulder on Hugh still standing by the window.

Kelly was into the room before Lindsay had finished speaking. 'Helloo . . .' She smiled enchantingly at Hugh, then flashed an expectant glance at Lindsay.

'Hugh Rydon, Kelly Jordan,' Lindsay muttered.

'Hello, Kelly.' Hugh returned Kelly's smile in the way most men did, Lindsay supposed a little tartly. But then, why should Hugh Rydon be an exception? And then they all just stood there.

'Am I interrupting?' Kelly looked at Lindsay like a charmingly embarrassed child. 'I'll pop in later, shall I?' she offered, the tension in the atmosphere too thick for even Kelly to miss.

'You're not interrupting anything, Kelly,' Lindsay assured her quickly. 'Mr . . . Hugh was just leaving, weren't you?' She showed her teeth at him.

'Look, I didn't mean to butt in,' Kelly started edging back towards the door.

'Not at all, Kelly,' Hugh forestalled her, leaving his place by the window and coming to their end of the room so that the three of them were bunched up by the door. 'I really am leaving,' he confirmed Lindsay's last statement with a wry smile. 'But Lindsay would appreciate some company. She's just out of hospital, you see, and I know you won't mind keeping a friendly eye on her.' He smiled again, with point-scoring malice, as Lindsay was momentarily struck speechless by his presumption. 'I'll be in touch, Lindsay. Take care of yourself.'

'Wow!' Kelly breathed, rapt, as Lindsay slammed the door shut on him with a viciousness that made it rattle. She spun her eyes to Lindsay. 'Now, tell me what happened? What accident? Have you really been in hospital? And who was that gorgeous man?' She flung the questions one after another without pause for breath or answer, then grinned sheepishly. 'Sorry. Are you all right? You do look worn out. Why don't you lie down on the bed and . . .'

'Don't you start!' Lindsay burst out, her temper hanging by a thread, and then saw the perplexed hurt in Kelly's eyes. 'Oh, hell, Kelly, I didn't mean to snap, and yes, I think I will lie down. I'm all right, so please don't fuss. I've a little headache—an ordinary headache,' she added as Kelly's eyes bore into the plaster on her temple as if it had suddenly begun to gush blood.

'What sort of accident, Lindsay? Did someone assault you?' Kelly asked worriedly.

Lindsay gave a dry laugh. 'No. I wasn't coshed on the head, I just didn't see a bus as I darted across the street on Friday afternoon. Someone pulled me out of the way but I fell and hit my head on the kerb, which is why I've got the bruises and the gash under the plaster. I also had a bit of concussion, which is why I spent the weekend in hospital. OK . . .?'

'Oh.' Kelly's voice held a tinge of disappointment that the accident had been so unexciting, after all.

Lindsay took off her coat, dropped it over the chair and then eased herself down on to the bed, stretching out full-length. 'That's better,' she said as her head settled into the pillow.

'Can I telephone anyone for you? Your mother?' Kelly offered anxiously.

'Don't be daft,' Lindsay said with a snap. 'Thanks anyway, but it's nothing to worry anyone about.' She wished Kelly would go away and leave her in peace, only she couldn't think of a way of telling her without being more rude than she already was.

'He was awfully nice, your friend.'

Fishing by any other name. Lindsay smiled faintly up at her, not biting, but she said, 'I think he thought you were awfully nice too,' and wondered that she should remember so vividly how Hugh's face had lit up when he'd smiled at Kelly.

'Do you?' Kelly sounded thrilled, hopeful—then sighed lavishly. 'Not my type, unfortunately. Too sophisticated. Yours. Have you known him long?'

'No,' Lindsay said shortly, letting Kelly's preposterous assessment of her 'type' pass without comment.

'Mind my own business, huh? OK.' Kelly grinned. 'Why don't you get undressed and put yourself to bed properly? I can bring up some takeaway for supper if you like, and I'll ask Mrs Layton to look in on you later when I go out, shall I?'

'Fine,' Lindsay agreed, ready to agree to anything.

The quiet was bliss after Kelly's exuberant presence . . . after Hugh Rydon's tension-charged presence. Lindsay got up, undressed and slipped in between the sheets. She felt drained, and it wasn't just physical; her mind felt as if it had really been run over by a bus, unable to take in all the things Hugh had told her about Charles, let alone all the things Hugh had implied about her—that she was a would-be suicide, on top of a blackmailing ex-mistress. No, it was just neurotic ex-mistress now, Lindsay amended with grim fury; she had been cleared of the blackmail. She ground her teeth savagely as she stared up at the dingy ceiling. Why couldn't she laugh about it? It was funny enough, wasn't it? No, it wasn't, and that was the problem; she felt hurt and humiliated that Hugh had made such hideous assumptions about her.

Her type, indeed! Kelly needed her head read. Even under the most ordinary circumstances—say, meeting him at a party—Hugh Rydon was the sort of man any sane woman would run a mile from. Sophisticated, yes, but as arrogant as they came, and just as cynical, judging by his casual dismissal, if not actual acceptance, of his cousin's philandering ways. And altogether too attractive. Too . . . male—a maleness every woman seemed to respond to willy-nilly . . . the nurses . . . Maree . . . Kelly. Lindsay smiled sourly. But not me, she congratulated herself, before her own nerve-tingling response to him in the car came back to her . . . the consciousness of his closeness and the irrational sense of vulnerability she had felt. An instinctive sexual reaction, and Lindsay didn't like it. Wasn't used to it. She had always been in control of her reactions, of her interaction with a man, and somehow Hugh Rydon had threatened that control. But he wouldn't get the chance to do it again because she wasn't going to be seeing him again, she reassured herself, drifting off to sleep, and only surfacing when Mrs Layton, the manageress, came in, avid for details of the accident, which Lindsay suspected Kelly had worked up into a near catastrophe.

There was no Ruytons courier with the pendant the next day. Lindsay spent the day waiting in her room, feeling better enough to be bored by the inactivity when she wasn't fuming that Hugh hadn't kept his word about the opal—implied word, albeit; he hadn't exactly said he would return it immediately, but he had given her to understand that it was out of Charles' hands and on Ruytons' premises ready to be returned to her.

Then, when Maree trundled up the stairs very late in the afternoon, Lindsay thought it had arrived at last. She was wrong. Maree had only come to pass on a message that a 'Mr Rydon' had telephoned to ask how she was, but had insisted she wasn't to be called downstairs to the telephone. Mrs Layton had spoken to him, Maree told her, and Lindsay could just imagine the drama the kindly busybody of a manageress would have made of her spending the day resting on her bed.

She shrugged off the message with a surly lift of the shoulder and wondered what Hugh thought he was going to achieve with his gratuitous concern, which didn't impress her one jot. He could keep his enquiries about her health; all she wanted from him was the pendant, and if it didn't show up by lunch the next day, she would go into Ruytons personally and demand it.

Or should she take a Ruytons cheque and let them have it? 'The money, darling, take the money,' Lindsay could hear her mother exhorting her. Maggie would very definitely want the money—and the kudos of having sold something to Ruytons. She had wanted that herself. Did she still, in spite of everything that had happened . . .? The small flicker of professional ambition made Lindsay waver, and she was still as undecided the next afternoon when she set out with Kelly for her friend's long-threatened raid on Oxford Street, returning hours later with nothing resolved—except Kelly's new wardrobe.

At least one of them was pleased with herself. Kelly was laden with about half a dozen carrier bags which she refused to let Lindsay help carry.

'You've got to take it easy, remember?' she admonished her, quite overlooking the fact that, having had the stamina to survive four hours of shopping with Kelly, Lindsay could have survived the weight of a carrier bag or two.

'Letter for you, Lindsay,' Maree called her over to the reception desk as they came in through the glass doors into the foyer, Lindsay first, Kelly trailing in after her.

'Thanks.' Lindsay took the letter from Maree's

outstretched hand and glanced at it, expecting to
see an airmail envelope with Australian stamps and
Maggie's scrawl—the expected follow-up to her
mother's telegram.

Beside her, Kelly flicked a curious eye over it
before Lindsay hurriedly rammed it out of sight
into her coat pocket.

'Ruytons?' Kelly's one thrilled word held a
dozen questions.

'It came by special courier,' Maree told her,
curious too, and making no bones about it. Her
eyes were intent on Lindsay's flushed face, and
Lindsay had the feeling her status had shot up
remarkably since she'd walked into the place with
Hugh Rydon at her side on Monday.

'Thanks,' she said again, curtly, and headed for
the stairs. A cheque for the opal? Nothing else it
could be. Well, that was a decision taken out of her
hands, and for the moment Lindsay was too
relieved to be annoyed at Hugh Rydon making the
decision for her.

'Aren't you going to open it?' Kelly asked
breathlessly, two steps behind her. 'It's from
Hugh, isn't it? He is *the* Rydon of Ruytons, isn't
he?' Kelly could put two and two together as well
as the next person. 'I thought he was when you
introduced us the other day. I've seen oodles of
photos of him in the social pages, and . . .'

The climb up the four flights had never seemed
so long, nor Kelly's blithe chatter more irritating.
Lindsay couldn't even pretend to listen. She
couldn't wait to get inside her room and rip the

envelope open.

'I'll catch up with you later.' Kelly took the silent hint and left at the top of their landing.

'Yes. Fine, see you later,' Lindsay returned distractedly, and, once inside her room, pulled out the letter but didn't rip it open. She stared at it.

The Ruytons logo in the top left-hand corner was as elegantly understated as everything else about it—except its owner; there was nothing at all understated about Hugh Rydon.

Slowly, Lindsay prised the flap up and drew out the sheet of thick, creamy paper. No cheque, she noted mechanically, and ran her eyes over the letter. Then she read it again, slowly, word by word almost. And again. Then she gave a short, stunned laugh and went and sat down on the edge of the bed and stared at the letter in disbelief.

A job. As a designer. With a special brief to initiate a range of jewellery featuring opals, and would she contact the office with regard to a meeting to discuss terms of employment, etc? Lindsay lowered the letter to her lap with shaking hands.

Exactly as Charles had promised, only the signature at the bottom of the page was Hugh Rydon's. Lindsay laughed again at the sheer absurdity of it. One day Hugh was patronisingly offering her a job as salesgirl, two days later . . . But why? He didn't know a thing about her. Oh, yes, she had told him she was a good designer—a damned good designer, she had flung at him, and she was, with several awards to prove it, but that was in Australia, and while Charles had seen examples of her work and had been impressed, it was Hugh who ran Ruytons, not Charles. For all he knew, her talents might be non-existent. But he would have spoken to Charles, Lindsay reasoned—doubtfully, since from the dismissive way Hugh had referred to his cousin, it was unlikely he would value Charles' opinion—of anything—very highly.

The disbelief . . . bewilderment was slowly giving way to a throbbing excitement. Ruytons . . . All the magic the name usually conjured up for her came flooding back in a wave of pure exhilaration. Designing for Ruytons . . . virtually given a *carte blanche* to use Maggie's splendid stones and create beautiful settings for them—light years away from the claws as big as shark's teeth and the 'the more, the better' school of dreary conventional design the wonderful stones seemed to have been doomed to for years.

Letter in hand, Lindsay jumped from the bed and stood at the window, watching a faint shaft of sunlight suddenly bathe the forlorn-looking garden in soft light. Her mind ran on at a hundred miles an hour . . . she could move out of this cubby-hole . . . find a small flat . . . perhaps ask Kelly to share with her.

She read the letter again, although she could have probably chanted off every word by heart. It wasn't a hoax. It was real—as real as Hugh Rydon himself.

And then everything changed and her excitement

vanished like the wintry sun behind the dark, scudding clouds. Hugh Rydon thought she was the sort of woman who had casual affairs with married men; who wasn't above trying a spot of blackmail; who was neurotic enough to hurl herself under a bus. And then he had the nerve to offer her a job? No, thank you, Mr Rydon. She wouldn't take his job if her life depended on it.

Very quickly, Lindsay tore up the letter and tossed the pieces into the waste-paper basket, then, picking up the elegant envelope from the bed, she glanced at it with distaste, and tore it up into a dozen little pieces too.

CHAPTER FOUR

LINDSAY went to the local doctor the next afternoon to have the plaster removed and the cut inspected as the hospital had told her to do. The young doctor recommended by Mrs Layton had done just that—removed the plaster and pronounced the small cut healing nicely. Lindsay could have worked that out for herself; there was barely a mark where the couple of stitches had been.

After that, she went for a desultory stroll up Oxford Street again, not particularly interested in anything, and certainly not in the dress shops; after the previous day's foray with Kelly, she felt she never wanted to see another rack of clothes as long as she lived. She was just killing time, wandering about trying not to think . . . about Ruytons . . . Hugh Rydon . . . getting the pendant back.

She had not acknowledged receipt of his letter and didn't intend to, and it gave her a sour satisfaction knowing that Hugh Rydon would have expected her to hare to the telephone the instant she read his letter. Hah! One in the eye for him, Lindsay thought smugly, but the satisfaction was short-lived and hollow, because one small part of her kept begging her to telephone and accept the job. Who cared if Hugh thought her a promiscuous, conscienceless neurotic? She did, that was who.

Kelly wasn't back yet from her first 'big-time' agency interview when Lindsay returned to the hotel. She had seen her friend off just after lunch, excited, scared—and looking fabulous. And far too preoccupied to even think about asking about Ruytons' letter. With a bit of luck, she would be too wildly excited when she got back to remember it, or start wondering what Lindsay herself was doing about jobs.

What was she going to do? Lindsay couldn't think past getting the opal back and catching the first plane home to Australia, yet at the back of her mind she knew her pride wouldn't let her do that. There were other reputable jewellers in London, and surely one of them was going to be interested in her? She was 'a damned good designer', and she wasn't going to let herself forget it.

Lindsay went down a floor to the small kitchenette the long-term guests were permitted to use, made herself a cup of tea, and was only just back in her room when Mrs Layton herself huffed up the stairs to tell her she was wanted on the telephone.

'Is it Kelly?' Lindsay asked, thinking Kelly might be ringing to suggest meeting up somewhere for a drink—a celebratory one, she hoped.

'A gentleman,' Mrs Layton wheezed. She was dreadfully overweight and the climb had winded her. 'Your friend, Mr Rydon,' she managed to get out in between gasps.

Which explained how she had been persuaded up the stairs at all—Hugh Rydon's unfailing charm. 'You haven't told him I'm in, have you?' Lindsay demanded, suspecting the worst.

'Yes, dear, I have. I saw you come in earlier, remember . . .?' Mrs Layton paused for breath, studying Lindsay sternly. 'And I've told Mr Rydon as much so you'd better come down and not ask me to make a liar of myself as I rather think you want me to,' the manageress told her, all in one burst.

Lindsay pinkened at having her mind read so shrewdly. 'Very well. Thank you,' she said stiffly, and followed Mrs Layton down the stairs in silence.

The extension for the guests' use was at the end of the foyer near the staircase. It had no provision for privacy, and was simply the instrument plonked on a small wooden stand. Anybody could listen in to anybody, if they wanted.

'I've already put the call through,' Mrs Layton told her. 'Since I knew you were in,' she tagged on self-righteously.

Lindsay waited until the woman had returned behind the reception desk, which she manned when Maree left for the day, before picking up the receiver. 'Lindsay Warren,' she said curtly, trying to keep her voice low to stop it floating across the foyer.

'Hello, Lindsay, it's Hugh. Rydon,' Hugh added as a formal afterthought.

Lindsay's hand tightened around the instrument at the warm, husky voice in her ear—intimately warm, and it sent an involuntary tingle shooting down the back of her neck. 'Yes, Mr Rydon?' she said, making her own voice ice-cold in hostile contrast to Hugh's warmth.

In the short pause she could picture the scowl—and Mrs Layton's ears flapping.

'I thought we'd dispensed with formalities, Lindsay. How are you?' Hugh asked, carefully keeping his voice pleasant.

'Fine, thank you,' Lindsay returned tersely.

'That's good.'

'Yes, isn't it?' she retorted shakily, and listened to another prolonged silence.

'Mrs Layton told me you'd just come back from the doctor . . . Did you get my letter yesterday?' Hugh let the testiness come through as he dispensed with the fatuous pretence that he'd telephoned to discuss her health.

'Yes.'

'And . . .?'

'And nothing,' Lindsay snapped.

'Now what is that supposed to mean?' Hugh snapped back.

'It means,' she enunciated distinctly, 'that I am not interested in your job. Thank you for the offer, but no, thanks.'

She waited for the angry protest, but there wasn't any. 'I think we need to talk about it, Lindsay,' he said with the note of conciliatory patience adults use when a child is about to throw a tantrum.

'And I think we've done all the talking we need

to, Mr Rydon. All I want to know is when I can expect my opal back. You said . . .'

'Have dinner with me tonight,' he cut in abruptly.

'No.'

'I'll pick you up at seven-thirty.'

'No!' Lindsay repeated sharply—to the burring sound in her ear. 'Hugh! Don't you dare!' she called out in an angry yell that must have all but pierced Mrs Layton's eardrums. 'Damn,' she muttered and banged down the receiver with an infuriated slam.

'Finished already, dear?' asked Mrs Layton, who was just happening to be walking across the foyer.

Lindsay tossed her a scowl. Wasn't anyone entitled to any privacy in this so-called Private Hotel? If it wasn't Maree, it was the manageress—not to mention Kelly, although Kelly's interest . . . curiosity . . . was forgivable, their early exchange of confidences and hopes rendering them friends. Besides, Kelly was a dear. So was Mrs Layton, for that matter, only, dear or not, she had a nose like a ferret for her guests' business.

Now what? Lindsay flicked a scowl at her watch. Five-thirty. She could go out, of course, disappear for the evening, but instinct told her that, no matter how long she stayed out, she'd find Hugh waiting on the doorstep whatever time she returned.

What on earth did the man want from her?

Lindsay couldn't work it out. Ruytons didn't need
an opal collection to enhance their reputation—
and they certainly didn't need her, an unknown
from Australia, her work so 'modern', most
conventional jewellers would have needed to think
very hard before taking her on. And now, here was
Ruytons all but pestering her to take a job with
them. Not Ruytons—Hugh Rydon; he was the one
who wanted her, Lindsay was sure of it. What she
couldn't fathom, though, was why. Well, the
dinner should prove the answer to that—and the
opportunity to tell Mr Rydon what he could do
with his job.

Lindsay went to take a bath. It was one of the
things she hated most about the hotel—sharing a
bathroom, and not a shower in the place. 'Baths
are so much more relaxing, aren't they, dear?' Mrs
Layton had cooed when Lindsay had first asked if
there was a shower she might use in one of the
other bathrooms. Relaxing, my foot, she thought,
giving herself a quick swish with the perennially
lukewarm water which seemed to have an in-built
tendency to run out at about four inches.

Then she spent an inordinately long time getting
ready. 'Just because,' she muttered to herself when
she couldn't come up with a reason for taking such
pains over a date that had been forced on her. The
black cashmere dress had long sleeves and a very
smooth, slinky line to it, skimming her body to the
knees. The conventional 'little black', and
simplicity itself, costing an arm and a leg and
looking the proverbial million dollars. Black

suited Lindsay, and the beaded leaf motif coming down from one shoulder softened the austerity; so did the shoulder-length hair framing her face instead of being drawn tightly away from it in its usual severe style which would have shown the faint bruising.

Black silk stockings; high heels. In for a penny . . . Lindsay shrugged and put on make-up: eyeshadow, mascara, blusher—the works, adding a few dabs of some superb duty-free perfume for good measure. Then, with her coat draped over her shoulders, she was downstairs in the foyer at seven-fifteen so that Hugh wouldn't get the chance to come to her tiny room and fill it with his too-male presence, setting off those disturbing feelings of hurt defensiveness and the irrational vulnerability that she found threatening as much as annoying.

'Wow!'

Kelly's highest accolade. Lindsay grinned as Kelly came swirling in through the swinging glass doors—a vision of mulit-layers of black and white. 'Lindsay, you look stunning.' Kelly went exaggeratedly goggle-eyed. 'Stunning!'

Lindsay laughed, ludicrously pleased. 'Thanks.'

'Hugh . . .?' Kelly hit the only nail on the head.

Lindsay gave a small nod. 'How did the agency interview go?' she put in quickly, to pre-empt any follow-up questions.

'Terrific. Tell you about it tomorrow. Have a lovely time,' Kelly sang out over her shoulder as she bounded towards the stairs, while at the other end of the foyer the glass doors swung open again and Hugh strode in. Early, by about twelve minutes, Lindsay noted.

'Hello, there.' Kelly waved at him from the stairs.

Smiling, Hugh raised a hand in a quick hello, but his eyes were on Lindsay. So were Mrs Layton's. Lindsay was very conscious of the beady eyes trained on them from the reception desk, which was possibly why she smiled so brilliantly at Hugh, disconcerting him as much as herself, and heaven only knew what Mrs Layton made of it.

'You're looking very well,' Hugh said in understatement of the look of obvious, if surprised, admiration in his eyes. 'And very lovely.' His smile seemed to lodge in the grey depths of his eyes, lighting them up with a glow that sent a sudden thrill through Lindsay and made her catch her breath.

She flushed madly at the compliment, the smile, and her own brief, silly reaction. 'Thanks,' she muttered, flusteredly reminding herself that a warm, admiring smile of appreciation of her looks didn't take away anything from Hugh Rydon's very low opinion of her in every other respect. 'Shall we go?' she suggested brusquely, and started towards the door.

'I'm sorry I haven't had the chance to get home to change. I'm straight from the office,' Hugh explained away his business suit with an apologetic smile as he helped her into the car in the absence of the driver, who apparently wasn't required for his employer's social activities. Social, or business?

Lindsay was not sure what this date was all about—nor the twittery feeling in the pit of her stomach.

She lifted a dismissive shoulder without comment. Hugh looked better than most men deserved to at any time, let alone after a day in the office. And he probably knew it.

'I see the plaster has come off. Everything all right now?' His hand on the ignition key, Hugh turned to her, taking a long, assessing look that instantly had Lindsay's own hand shooting up to her hair and drawing it further over her cheek.

'Fine, thanks,' she replied with discouraging frostiness, angrily self-conscious about the barely noticeable bruising.

And that put an end to that. They drove in silence, but not very far. In fact, they could probably have walked to the restaurant, which was only a block or two from the hotel, tucked down one of those quaint little streets so typical of London, and which you came across accidentally, rather than by design. The restaurant was like that, too—the sort of place you had to know was there in the first place. It was very small and unpretentious—and quietly expensive—yet something about its clientèle and general ambience suggested that its drawing power was simply good food, not trendiness. Something also told Lindsay that Hugh was not out to impress as Charles would have been; they were here because he liked it and evidently came often, judging from the easy friendliness of the host as he took Lindsay's coat and led them to their table.

They were still silent when the drinks waiter brought back their order—a small whisky for Hugh, mineral water for Lindsay. She was determined to keep a clear head for when Hugh got around to breaking the leaden silence and beginning on whatever he had up his sleeve—bullying her into taking the job, she presumed, on guard and ready for anything until Hugh said, ever so casually, 'I spoke with your mother the other day,' and floored her completely.

'When was it, now . . .?' He furrowed his brow in concentration as Lindsay stared in blank astonishment. 'Monday, I think,' he went on with a vagueness that didn't fool her for a moment, and he smiled quizzically across the table at her, eyes sharply alert in contrast to his smile as they waited for her reaction.

Lindsay put down her glass with a clatter. 'How dare you take it upon yourself to telephone my mother?' she demanded in a shaking undertone, her self-control stretched to the limit in the effort not to yell at him. 'My accident was none of your business, and my mother has enough worries without your twisted conclusions about a perfectly ordinary accident which could have happened to anybody. I've had enough of your interference, Mr Rydon.' Lindsay was pushing back her chair as she spoke, the evening over as far as she was concerned.

She thought the hand was just lifting in a gesture of protest until it shot past the centre-piece of flowers between them and Hugh's fingers snapped around her wrist like a handcuff, holding it hard down to the table.

'I haven't finished yet, Lindsay,' he told her quietly, and without making a scene she was trapped.

Lindsay sat there glaring an impotent fury as they held hands in a parody of a pair of lovers, taking in the Italian waiter at least, who nodded them an approving smile as he brought their smoked salmon to the table and then stood hovering until Hugh reluctantly released her wrist to make room for the dishes.

She could have got up then and left. Lindsay decided against it: her initial paroxysm of fury over, she had a lot to say to her handsome, presumptuous dinner companion.

Hugh got it first. 'It seems I'm not the only one prone to jumping to conclusions,' he began as soon as the waiter left. 'And surely you could credit me with more tact that worrying your mother about your accident?'

'Tact?' Lindsay scoffed with a little cackle. 'You wouldn't even know how to spell it.'

'I didn't mention your accident,' Hugh ignored her interjection, 'and as for having jumped to the wrong conclusion about it, I apologise. You are very definitely not the suicidal type, and I don't know how I ever thought you were.' He smiled in wry apology, which meant absolutely nothing to Lindsay.

She made a hrumphing sort of growl, relieved Maggie hadn't been sent out of her wits by an attempted suicide tale, but too angry to be mollified by Hugh's change of opinion about that particular trait of her character. 'Are you about to tell me you telephoned my mother for the pleasure of a chat?' Lindsay queried in acid disbelief.

'No. I rang Maggie to assure her she would receive a banker's order for the pendant. And,' he ran on firmly as Lindsay opened her mouth to tell him he should have consulted her first. 'And,' Hugh repeated, eyeing her steadily, 'to discuss her terms of trade regarding the opals Ruytons will be needing to buy in for your designs. Maggie was delighted at the prospect of doing business with us,' he added with sly satisfaction.

Lindsay sat back, shaking her head at him, not knowing whether to rant, laugh or storm out. 'You would have to be the most presumptuous, most devious man I have ever met—your cousin doesn't come anywhere near you,' she said at last, still shaking her head in semi-feigned incredulity.

'Thank you.' Hugh's eyes went suddenly hard. 'I'll take that as a compliment, shall I—that I'm unlike my cousin . . .?'

'Take it any way you like,' Lindsay snapped, exasperated, 'but I'm not taking your job. And if you think you can coerce me into it by buying some of Maggie's opals, you've another think coming. You can buy all the opals you like and stud your teeth with them for all I care.'

Hugh smiled faintly. 'Your mother will be disappointed. She was very pleased to hear Ruytons had offered you a job.' He took a mouthful of his salmon and chewed solemnly. 'Hmmm. Delicious. You haven't tried yours yet,' he pointed out solicitously.

The laugh jolted itself out of her . . . amusement . . . anger . . . and sheer helplessness. The man was impossible. Lindsay attacked her salmon with repressed frustration, staying silent while she ate, and sipping the delicious dry white wine almost with abandon, because it really didn't matter about keeping a clear head any more. Clear or fuzzy-headed, she simply wasn't a match for Hugh Rydon.

'Why?' she asked suddenly when she had finished and the plates had been cleared away. 'Why are you trying to bully me into taking this job?'

'Am I bullying?' Hugh affected injured surprise.

'Yes, you are, and you know it. Only I don't understand why, so you tell me.'

'Because you're good,' Hugh said simply, and startled her into one, tiny, gratified moment before she realised it was only flattery.

'I know that,' Lindsay muttered, angry, 'but how do you?'

Hugh shrugged. 'I've seen the pendant, but, more to the point, Charles vouches for your talent—designing talent, that is,' he qualified carefully, meeting her eyes expressionlessly. Lindsay felt her face warming and dropped her eyes hurriedly. 'Charles is the artistic one of the family,' Hugh went on, making the description sound like a disease. 'And since I have no talent in that direction myself, I take his advice when it comes to designers, designs and suchlike. I merely look after the business—doing unartistic things like buying in the gems, paying staff and generally seeing to it that our artists don't send us broke.' There was a smile in his voice. Lindsay looked up with unwilling interest at Hugh's mocking self-assessment. It was true: no one could possibly mistake him for an artist of any description. There was something much too substantial . . . too feet-on-the-ground about him. A businessman.

'Edwards, our head designer and workshop manager, also thinks you've got what it takes,' Hugh said, and it didn't sound as if he was flattering her. 'He's interested in seeing your designs. You've brought them with you, haven't you?'

Lindsay nodded before she could think.

'Then what about coming in on Monday? Come on, Lindsay,' Hugh cajoled with an impatient laugh. 'You'd give your eye-teeth to be designing for Ruytons, so why pretend you don't want the job?'

'I'm not pretending. I . . . oh, you wouldn't understand.' And she couldn't tell him he was the reason she couldn't take the job.

'Charles,' Hugh stated with sudden harshness. 'That's why you're digging your heels in, isn't it?'

'No,' Lindsay denied sharply, and could see from the way Hugh's mouth went all grim and disapproving that he didn't believe her.

'I told you he's back from Paris. Do you want to see him?' The grey eyes bored into her face unwaveringly, not about to miss the minutest flicker of expression.

Linday met them impassively. 'No, I don't,' she said firmly with a shake of the head.

'Then for heaven's sake, Lindsay, put him out of your mind,' Hugh broke out irritably. 'Look,' he continued after a moment of just staring at her, 'you won't have to come across him often, just once in a while when he comes in to discuss new collections with Edwards. Surely you can cope with that?' he asked testily. 'And anyway, you'll have to get over him sooner or later, so you may as well nerve yourself and make it sooner. Have it out with him if you need to, and . . .'

'I do not need to!' Lindsay almost bellowed at him. 'Any more than I need your advice to the love-lorn, so cut it out, will you? And yes, damn it, I will take the job,' she finished with a growl and no awareness that she had done an about-turn in her mind. Then she had to grin in spite of herself at what surely must have been the most ungracious acceptance of a job on Ruytons' books.

Hugh seemed momentarily taken by surprise, but then his laugh resounded around the small room, turning smiling faces towards them. 'I must say I had no idea recruiting staff was so difficult. I must give Mrs Buchanan a raise if this is what she's up against. Mrs Buchanan is my deputy and deals with staff administration,' he explained. 'You'll meet her on Monday.'

'We've met,' Lindsay said, without elaborating.

The rest of the dinner was almost a date in the conventional sense of the world. 'Business' out of the way, Hugh put himself out to be an amusing and interesting companion. Laid on the charm, Lindsay would have said, if she hadn't been beguiled by it, her defences temporarily down as she listened, fascinated, to the 'inside' history of Ruytons' beginnings . . . how Hugh's great-grandfather had come from Holland in the previous century to set up the family concern. Charles had already told her some of the story, but Charles had mainly concentrated on Charles, whereas Hugh filled in the gaps and seemed to want her to feel part of the company she was about to join.

Basically, it was a safe, unthreatening subject, and then, somehow, Lindsay was telling him about her own family—about her father's death in the opal fields fifteen years ago when a wall of the shaft he had dug collapsed on him. He had been a typical opal miner, fascinated—obsessed with the wondrous stones which in the end cost him his life, leaving Maggie with a small child to bring up alone.

The fascination, if not obsession with opals ran in the family. Maggie had left the opal fields to start up an opal wholesale business, eventually becoming one of the most respected dealers in the country.

'With that sort of background, is it any wonder I ended up a designer?' Lindsay finished with a laugh, and then, as her laugh died she became conscious how much Hugh had drawn out from her over their after-dinner coffee and port. 'Are you always so thorough in learning about your employees' background?' she smiled.

Hugh smiled back through half-lidded eyes. 'Only with some of them,' he said, his voice low and husky, sending an instant tautness through her and starting warning bells clanging in her head.

CHAPTER FIVE

LINDSAY'S hand was already reaching for the door-handle as they drew up just along the street from the entrance to her hotel—the closest parking spot in the small street chock-a-block full of cars. It has been an unnerving drive home. The air of relaxed companionship that had settled in during the second half of the dinner had vanished, for Lindsay at any rate, with Hugh's last smile: too warm, too intimate, and infinitely threatening, it catapulted her back into defensiveness and an anger with herself for having succumbed to the charm that obviously ran—in torrents—through the male line of Rydons.

Hugh chatted on and Linday made the odd distracted remark, but she was tense and on edge, and then, as they rounded the last corner, had an attack of the sort of idiotic jitters teenagers had coming home with their first date. Was Hugh going to try to make a pass . . .?

'Don't bother seeing me in, thanks,' Lindsay muttered quickly. 'And thank you for the dinner. I . . . What are you doing?' She swung her eyes back to him as Hugh reached over and whipped her hand away from the door-handle. 'Let me go,' she ordered when he held on to her hand, tightly, smiling drily at her agitation.

'What's the rush?' His smile looked foxy in the light coming into the car from the streetlamp beside them.

Lindsay couldn't answer that without sounding an idiot. 'Please let go of my hand,' she said crossly.

'Only if you promise not to bolt out the door like a frightened rabbit. What are you afraid of, Lindsay?' Hugh asked with soft menace.

'Don't be silly, Hugh.' Lindsay gave her hand a tug and Hugh released it with an amused laugh.

'About Monday. Would ten o'clock suit you for coming in?' he said briskly, and Lindsay felt a fool.

She gave a silly little giggle in her relief that Hugh only wanted to discuss business, not make the dreaded pass. 'Yes, of course. Ten o'clock will be super,' she trilled, very brightly.

'Good. Then go into the Gallery and ask Mr Barlow to take you to Mrs Buchanan. I'm afraid I'm leaving for a short business trip to the continent tomorrow and won't be back until around Thursday, but Mrs Buchanan will discuss salary and anything else with you, and then pass you on to Edwards,' Hugh instructed in the same businesslike voice. 'Did I tell you Edwards was very impressed with your pendant? He is really looking forward to seeing the drawings for your other designs.'

Edwards. Ruytons' chief designer . . . impressed? Looking forward to seeing her other designs . . .? Lindsay felt a warm glow wash over her.

'Do you have any idea how lovely you look when your eyes shine like that?' Hugh murmured, moving closer and with a look of open hunger in his eyes that stopped Lindsay's heart in its tracks and every thought in her head. The tremor that shot through her was nervous, excited anticipation as Hugh's eyes held her in that smouldering grey stare.

Lindsay's eyes widened as the dark head bent towards her, slowly, and then closed as their mouths came together. 'This is madness', was the last rational thought she was capable of thinking. She murmured a long half-sigh, half-groan and nestled into him as he wrapped an arm around her neck, curving his hand under her jaw to hold it up against the breaktaking pressure of his kiss.

Lindsay responded as if she had been waiting for this kiss all her life—hungrily . . . mindlessly, and then with an almost desperate edge to her passion when Hugh's mouth deliberately lessened the pressure and began to tease tantalisingly at her lips with soft, flickering kisses, arousing her to the point of dizziness but setting off ache after unsatisfied ache for harder, deeper probing.

She felt Hugh slipping his other hand into her unbuttoned coat and tensed involuntarily, then arched sensuously on a shuddery whimper of pure pleasure as the hand cupped her breast, thumb seeking out the hardened nipple and stroking it through the soft cashmere of her dress while his mouth at last resumed the breathtakingly deep probing that sent her senses spinning.

Lindsay's hand was in the act of reaching into his shirt, wanting to touch, run her fingers over warm, bare skin, when her mind came plummeting back to earth and jolted the madness right out of her. She pulled her hand—and mouth—away in the same violent wrench.

'What do you think you're doing?' Lindsay demanded in mortified blaze of accusation, barely able to get the words out for breathlessness, and barely able to look into the mildly surprised eyes under their preposterously long lashes.

'What are you?' Hugh countered softly. The hand around her neck slid down to her shoulder and stayed there, while the hand at her breast tightened with outrageous deliberateness around the soft curve. Hugh watched her face with a faintly amused smile.

'How dare you?' Lindsay gritted, thumping the hand away from her breast, but her angry shrugs couldn't dislodge the arm around her shoulder. 'Take your hand off me,' she ordered, furious.

Hugh gave a derisive laugh at her futile efforts. 'Come on, Lindsay, what's all this about? You enjoyed our kiss as much as I did, so why the belated 'outraged' act? We're both too sophisticated for that, don't you think?' he drawled, but a slight puzzlement was showing in his eyes as they ranged over her flushed face.

About as sophisticated as two teenagers having a necking session, but what Hugh said was true, and all the outrage in the world couldn't cover up the very obvious fact that for the space of a couple of mindless minutes Lindsay had loved the kiss . . . the touch of Hugh's hand on her breast. Only it didn't mean she didn't regret every insane moment of her passionate response, nor did it mean that she was the fair game Hugh assumed she was. And a dim-witted fifteen-year-old could have followed his facile reasoning: if she could have a fling with his cousin at the drop of a hat—or with the name 'Ruytons'—then she'd be a pushover for the man who really counted. Give her a job, and she'd be so grateful she'd . . .

'And I suppose since we're both so sophistiacted we'll now go up to my room and hop into bed to make a night of it?' Lindsay jeered icily.

'If that is an offer, I accept,' Hugh smiled with silky menace.

'Ha, ha,' Lindsay grated. 'And as for *your* offer of the job, I'm afraid I wasn't aware of the exact terms of employment when I accepted it, but now that you've made them clear to me, you can keep your job, Mr Rydon. I don't want it so badly that I'm prepared to accept your attached conditions.' Lindsay swung agitatedly towards the door, only to have the arm over her shoulder pull her roughly back to him.

'There aren't any conditions, you idiot,' Hugh growled at her, his face close, and eyes sparking with angry.

'Oh, no?' Lindsay challenged. 'And I suppose that was just a goodnight kiss?'

Hugh drew bag and stared for a moment as if he was having trouble working out what she meant. 'What else do you think it was, for God's sake?' he snapped, exasperated. 'You're a very attractive, very desirable woman. As if you didn't know,' he added with a short, gruff laugh. 'And it's certainly evident that you've been kissed before. So why make such an issue out of it now?'

'Because!' Lindsay retorted in frustrated, childish belligerence. Because somehow it seemed so dreadfully important she didn't confirm his mistaken assumption that she was the sort of woman who made herself available to every attractive man who came her way. Except of course that unintentionally she had confirmed it, and Hugh was right: her attack of belated indignation was plain silly. 'Let me go, Hugh. Please,' she asked wearily.

'You're still in love with him,' Hugh burst out with a verbal pounce as if he'd caught her out in something she was trying to hide from him, and Lindsay nearly laughed—might have, if Hugh hadn't looked so threatening all of a sudden, with a sense of barely suppressed violence about him. He took his arm off her shoulder abruptly and yanked open his door with a ferocity that sent it swinging on its hinges.

Lindsay scrambled out of the car and then tried to push him as Hugh reached her side just in time to block her next move.

'Lindsay . . . for God's sake,' Hugh's voice held a mixture of frustration and anger as he gripped her by both shoulders and pulled her hard to him, ramming his mouth down in a short, savage kiss that was over before she got over the surprise of it. 'The job is yours, no strings attached, take it or leave it,' he snarled and, dropping his hands, stormed back to the driver's side without another glance.

Lindsay stared after the receding tail-lights of the long, sleek limousine until they disappeared around the corner, then turned and walked slowly to the hotel, her mind too much of a whirl to even be grateful it was Mr Layton at the desk for the night, not his busybody wife. A short, stocky man, and uncommunicative to the point of dourness, he gave Lindsay an uninterested nod as he handed her her key.

'Take it or leave it,' Hugh had snarled, and Lindsay spent the night in sleepless, angry confusion, taking it one minute, leaving it the next . . . see-sawing between telling herself wild horses couldn't drag her into Ruytons again—or anywhere there was the remotest chance of coming across Hugh Rydon—and that she'd be the world's biggest idiot to turn her back on the opportunity of a lifetime just because she had made a fool of herself for a couple of minutes in his arms. It would never happen again, and since Hugh never came into the workshop, she wouldn't even need to see him.

Drowsily satisfied with that bit of reasoning, Lindsay dozed off and told Kelly the next day that she had been offered a job of Ruytons and was thinking about it.

'Thinking about it . . .? What's there to think about?' Kelly screeched. 'You've got to be joking, Lindsay. And that gorgeous man for a boss . . .? Wow!'

'He won't be my boss,' Lindsay pointed out with a snap. 'Not directly, anyway.'

'Pity,' Kelly grinned. 'But seriously, Lindsay, you can't be thinking of not accepting it?' Kelly sounded incredulous. 'I mean, it's what you've come to London for, isn't it?'

'Yes,' Lindsay agreed flatly. That was why she had followed Charles to London: to try her luck with Ruytons, whatever his cousin thought.

'And listen,' Kelly went on excitedly. 'Don't you see? If you take the job we could both move out of this dump sooner . . . get a flat together. The agency I saw yesterday is going to push me at their client for their new campaign. I'm sure to get the job. They're after someone sort of outrageous, and you couldn't get anyone more outrageous than me, could you?' Kelly appealed earnestly.

'Not without difficulty,' Lindsay conceded with a laugh. 'Oh, Kelly, I am sorry. I've been so caught up with my problems, I haven't even asked you about your interviews. Do you really think you'll get the job?'

'Bound to,' Kelly replied with easy confidence. 'My little face will be beaming at you from every Underground billboard as you hare along for your train. You'll hate the sight of me yet. It'll be wonderful . . .'

Lindsay listened for the next hour to Kelly's idea of heaven: commercials, magazines ads, posters— with Kelly featuring in every one for yet another new miracle shampoo the client had come up with.

'Yes, I'd love to share a flat,' Lindsay assured her when Kelly came down from the dizzy heights of her potential fame to more mundane matters, and knew that she would be walking into Ruytons on Monday morning. It had nothing to do with wanting a flat or wanting to stay on in London; it was a case of amibiton rearing its obstinate head, and exactly what Lindsay needed to put Hugh Rydon into perspective. Let him think what he wanted about her; it was her career that mattered, and all the Rydons in the world couldn't undermine her pride in that.

Oddly, the prospect of coming face to face with Charles again didn't disturb Lindsay in the slightest; cousin Hugh was the one to be avoided at all costs . . . a much more dangerous Rydon altogether, with his refined talent for getting under her skin.

The new girl at school, that was how Lindsay felt when, their session about terms and conditions over, the ever-elegant Mrs Buchanan took her into the large workshop at the end of the building and introduced her to the legendary Edwards. He was small and wiry, of indeterminate age and with round, pale eyes that took her in impassively, and a smile that looked as if it cost him a lot. From his manner, the last thing Lindsay would have gathered was that he had in any way been impressed by her work, or had any desire to see more of it.

There were three other people in the workshop —all men, Lindsay noted with surprise, two of them the sort of craftman featured in books on jewellery-making of thirty years ago. They gave her a nod as Edwards performed vague introductions, and only Philip, a sandy-haired young chap of about thirty, looked friendly, but she didn't get the chance to catch more than his name before Edwards whisked her away into his office and in no time flat put an end to her fantasy that she would swan in and start on 'her collection'.

In two hours they had only got through six of the drawings in her folio of about four dozen, and it didn't take Lindsay long to realise that if Edwards passed a dozen of them in total, she could consider herself lucky. Edwards shot questions at her about every aspect of her choice of shape, size, colour . . . she had to justify each stone for each ring, bracelet, pendant, and then found herself almost defending her approach in every design. It was frustrating exhausting, and surprisingly rewarding when Edwards gave one of his little nods of approval. And that wasn't very often.

Lindsay was never more relieved then when he finally suggested they break for lunch, but then, as she was about to leave, he picked up the top sketch and studied it again. It was a design for a pendant, its uncluttered, smooth line very similar to the black opal one, but where that was a swirl of heavy silver in the form of an elongated 'S' with only the single enormous black opal set into the tapering bottom of the 'S', this design was for a very slightly rounded neck-band—a collar almost, with a long piece coming down from the centre. Lindsay had decided on three opals either side of the centre, and three down the extension, all matching blue-green. It had a stark, but rather Byzantine effect, and she considered it the *pièce de résistance* of her folio.

'I've been thinking, Miss Warren . . . you might consider a focal stone here . . . at the point of meeting of collar and extension.' Edwards prodded the sketch with a thin, bony finger. 'Oh, yes, predictable, I know . . .' He smiled drily, and Lindsay could have sworn his eyes twinkled. 'But I would like you to think about it. Perhaps you would make up a model of the piece in the next week or so and then tell me how you feel about it. And perhaps also you might give some thought as to how other gems might fit into your designs—this, and others. Opals are very beautiful, Miss Warren, but some of our clients rather like a mix . . . the odd diamond . . . ruby . . .'

Was he telling her her designs were too . . . cheap . . . for Ruytons? Lindsay couldn't tell. She flushed slightly. 'And do you have something against claws, Miss Warren?' Edwards asked suddenly, and his eyes definitely twinkled this time.

'Yes, I do,' Lindsay returned unthinkingly. 'I mean . . . well . . . I . . .'

'So do I.' Edwards actually chuckled. 'However, they are often necessary, and sometimes very attractive, so do go a little easy in trying to avoid them, won't you? A designer can trap himself—I beg your pardon, herself—into styles as rigidly as the ones who can't design anything without a surfeit of claws.'

'Yes. I see.' Lindsay got out of Edwards' office at last, feeling like a first-year design student.

'How did you go with the master?' Philip grinned, waiting for her in the main workshop—empty during the lunch hour. 'Are you to sweep the workshop for a month before being promoted to clearing the work-benches?'

Lindsay laughed ruefully. 'I'm instructed to rethink a design—one design. At Edwards' pace I'll be an old woman by the time he lets me anywhere near a stone,' she groaned.

'Don't let it get you down. Come out for a spot of lunch—my treat for your first day. I'll take you to the café we usually go to, it's only a block or so away. Just grab your coat.'

Lindsay grabbed her coat and went out with Philip through the back exit, into an alley and along another which came out into a small street behind Bond Street.

'Working for Ruytons is the main thing,' Philip chatted on as they walked.' After a stint with them you'll be able to write your own ticket as a world-class designer,' he told her encouragingly as he led her into an Italian-type café.

'Should I live so long,' Lindsay muttered, only half-joking.

'Relax, old Edwards is just putting you through the hoops—testing your metal. Oops, sorry.' Philip guffawed at his excruciating pun. 'He did me too, if it's any consolation.' He broke off to give their order to the waiter, recommending the vegetable lasagne to Lindsay, who was so hungry she could have eaten the leg off the chair.

'Is everything done on the premises?' she asked when the waiter had gone. 'I didn't get a chance to look around, let alone take anything in.'

'I know,' Philip nodded with a chuckle. 'Doesn't believe in the guided tour, does he? No, we have another studio near Hatton Garden, and we also used specialist workshops for the non-custom-made stuff, as well as buying in things from certain high-class manufacturers and free-lancers too. A recent innovation, that, and all Hugh Rydon's doing. He yanked Ruytons—squealing, I might add—into the twentieth century when he took over about four . . . five years ago after his uncle died. That was Charles' father. Charles is not into business, so cousin Hugh took the chair. He used to run an electronics firm of some sort—still has an interest in it, I gather, which is why Ruytons' security system is second to none.' Philip told her more about Hugh in one breath than Hugh had done in a night. 'Know him well?' he suddenly shot at her.

'Hardly at all,' Lindsay replied shortly.

'Sorry,' Philip said quickly. 'Just wondered. You do know Charles, though, don't you? Madly artistic —trained as a designer himself and does all the final okaying with Edwards. He's great on PR and all that stuff, and is forever junketing around the world keeping an eye on trends. Well, you probably know all that.'

She knew all right. Lindsay murmured something indistinct.

'He was in last week—with your pendant, to show to Edwards. Great.' Philip's eyes shone with genuine admiration. 'Edwards was awfully impressed, although he wouldn't tell you that to save his life—nor yours,' he added, grinning. 'That pendant probably got you the job, otherwise you wouldn't have made first base with him if you'd been Mrs Hugh Rydon herself. Actually,' Philip continued thoughtfully, 'I wouldn't be surprised if Edwards doesn't really want you started on anything until the exhibition is over. You're bound to be doing some commission work after it, you see.'

'Exhibition?' Lindsay asked, deliberately vague to cover her surprise. 'Is it coming up soon?'

Philip nodded. 'In a couple of weeks. It's Charles' baby; ask him for the details when he comes into the workshop—Thursday, I think.'

So there really was to be an exhibition, and Charles hadn't strung her a line after all—about that at least, thought Lindsay, wryly amused, and then didn't give him another thought until he bounded into Edwards' office on Thursday afternoon when she and Edwards were just finishing another session of poring over her sketches.

'Lindsay . . .' Charles sprang across the room to her, arms outstretched, and even when Lindsay drew back from the threatened embrace, had the nerve to plant a kiss on her cheek, blithely uncaring of Edwards or other interested eyes trained on them through the glass wall that separated Edwards' office from the main workshop area. 'It's wonderful to see you again. And simply super to have you working with us,' he trilled, and certainly looked delighted. 'Well, Edwards, what do you think of my find? Fantastic, eh?'

Had he always used such an irritating stream of superlatives, or had she simply been too charmed to notice? Lindsay smiled, very tightly.

'Going over the designs? I simply must see them . . .' Charles reached to the folio open on Edwards' desk.

'Then I'll leave you to it,' Edwards said dourly. 'Feel free to make yourselves at home. I won't be needing my office for the rest of the afternoon.' He left—pointedly—and Lindsay wished she could have left with him.

Charles closed the door and leant back against it. 'Hello, Lindsay,' he greeted her again, softly and with a note of intimacy.

Lindsay looked back blandly. 'Hello, Charles,' she replied briskly.

'Well, I must say I didn't expect to see you in London quite so soon.'

'I imagine not,' Lindsay returned tartly.

'I say, Lindsay,' Charles looked sheepish, 'I'm awfully sorry about that cheque business, but I did so want to bring your pendant over for the exhibition and I thought I'd have time to transfer some funds into the account before . . .' he shrugged. 'Well, you know . . .'

'Before the cheque bounced,' Lindsay finished for him flatly, enjoying being a little mean.

'Sorry,' he repeated. 'Fact is, I forgot—what with one thing and another. Anyway, Hugh told me he has seen to it, so I'm sure Maggie has forgiven me.' Charles smiled disarmingly.

Only because Maggie didn't know what a ratfink he was, Lindsay thought, undisarmed. She hadn't bothered going into any details in the brief letter she had sent off to her mother earlier in the week.

'About . . . other things . . .' Charles pulled a wry face.

'Let's just forget it, shall we?' Lindsay suggested sharply.

'Oh, come on, now, Lindsay. I wouldn't want to

do that. We had a wonderful time, didn't we?'
Charles smiled with reminiscent warmth.

'How's your wife, Charles?' Lindsay wiped the
smile off his face, and wondered how she had ever
thought Charles Rydon the sophisticated, charming
man he thought himself. Charming, yes . . . a
charming, irresponsible, untrustworthy weakling.

'She's fine, thanks,' Charles muttered, abashed
for about two seconds. 'Honestly, Lindsay, no hard
feelings, eh . . . ? I didn't mean to hurt you.'

'You didn't,' Lindsay snapped, chagrined that he
could possibly think her heartbroken or whatever at
discovering he'd simply been a married man on the
loose.

'Anyway, it's great you're here. I'm glad Hugh has
seen to everything—hiring you and all that.'

It struck Lindsay that his reliance on Hugh's seeing
to everything was probably a habit of long-standing.

'What about a drink this evening? We've an awful
lot of catching up to do.' Charles was Charles again.

'Sorry. I'm busy,' Lindsay said airily. It happened
to be true, but she would have said it anyway, even if
she hadn't agreed to going for drinks with Philip.

'Oh. Right.' Charles nodded after a moment of
looking as if he was going to protest.' So, let's have a
look through the sketches, shall we?' he suggested,
very businesslike all at once. 'And, incidentally, we'll
have to get together with Edwards and make a final
decision about what we're going to buy in for you
from Maggie—not before the exhibition, though,
because my time is really cut out until that's over.'

Three weeks of flirtation vanished without a trace,

and so did Lindsay's mild hostility as they started going through the designs, temporarily colleagues, with Charles giving his opinion . . . making suggestions. And he was good; Lindsay recognised that immediately, and felt the tiniest bit more kindly towards him for it.

There was no tap on the door—or if there was, then neither of them heard it. The door suddenly just opened and Hugh walked in on them, startling them almost guiltily from the designs on the desk in front of them. They were leaning over Edwards' desk, side by side, their shoulders touching—a heart-warming sight if anyone chose to interpret it that way, and Hugh did. Lindsay could see that from his eyes as they looked them over, suspicion written all over his poker face.

She swerved her eyes past him, aware that she was flushing—not because of having been 'sprung' with Charles, but in searing recollection of those crazy moments in Hugh's arms on their last encounter.

'Hello, old chap,' Charles greeted his cousin with a bray of a laugh with sounded awfully embarrassed to Lindsay's ears, as if Charles, too, felt they had been sprung. Which was ludicrous, when they had absolutely nothing to feel embarrassed about.

'I didn't know you were in, Charles,' Hugh said coldly.

'Oh, then it must be Lindsay you've come to see . . .' Charles said airily, and to Lindsay's irritation he placed a hand on her shoulder, which might have been meant to indicate colleague-ly approval, but which was a gratuitously familiar gesture. The only

reason she didn't slap it off was because she was so
angry with Hugh for his disapproval at finding her
and Charles together, and she figured the hand on
the shoulder would annoy him more. She returned
her gaze to the hard, narrowed eyes focusing on the
scene in front of them.

'We've just been looking over some of Lindsay's
designs,' Charles told his cousin chattily, leaving the
offending hand firmly in place—very possibly with
the same intention as Lindsay in allowing it to stay
there.

'So Edwards told me,' Hugh muttered, glaring
hard at Charles and avoiding Lindsay's eyes.

'Ah, in which case you must have also known I'd
be here too, yes?' Charles caught his cousin out in the
curiously silly lie and enjoyed his point. 'I take it
you've only just got back yourself from wherever you
tycoons do your important business. You really do
look bushed, old boy,' he added with spurious
concern.

Now that Charles mentioned it, Lindsay could see
that Hugh did look tired. She had missed the strain
around the eyes in her first embarrassed glance, but
even so, he didn't look anywhere near as ready to
drop as Charles implied, and beside Charles' arty get-
up of toning greenish tweeds and flannel shirt, Hugh
looked as neat and crisp as if he'd just stepped out of
a board meeting, as he quite possibly had.

'You should take things a little easier,' Charles
went on like an old granny. 'I was only saying to
Natalie the other day that you seem to be out of the
country more often than in it these days. She wants

to see you, by the way.' There was a funny little undertone of malice in Charles' voice that Lindsay couldn't fathom. Hugh made no comment and Charles gave a shrug and a short, curious laugh. 'I don't suppose you've seen Lindsay's sketches yet? Come and take a look,' he invited, waving a hand at the drawings and at long last removing his other hand from Lindsay's shoulder.

'I'm sure I can leave the assessment of them to you, Charles,' Hugh declined the invitation stiffly. 'And when you've finished, perhaps you wouldn't mind coming up to my office, Lindsay,' he addressed his first words to her since walking into the room—his first words to her since the awful ending to their 'date', and they were an order to an employee, never mind the 'perhaps . . . wouldn't mind' business.

Lindsay was tempted to snap, 'Yes, sir, certainly, sir,' but somehow felt that Charles would have enjoyed the sarcasm at his cousin's expense, so just gave a small nod without saying anything, and after another sour look at both of them Hugh went out, closing the door with a restrained slam.

Charles turned to her and laughed. 'Probably wants you to take the company oath of allegiance. It's all right, I am joking,' he chuckled, 'although what he does want you up there for, I can't guess— nor what he was doing down here, for that matter. This is a foreign country as far as cousin Hugh is concerned. He wouldn't know a pearl from a diamond.'

'I hardly think that's true, since he does happen to run the business,' Lindsay rose snappily to Hugh's defence.

Charles raised an ironic eyebrow at her. 'So he does,' he agreed carelessly. 'So don't let me keep you. You'd better go up and see what the boss wants. We can get together on these another time.'

Lindsay gathered the sketches and put them back into the folder to take out with her.

'Leave them. I'd like to run through them later this evening, if I may. Sure you won't have a drink with me? For old times' sake?' Charles smiled one of his most persuasive smiles, which didn't do a thing for her—except irritate.

'Don't be silly, Charles,' Lindsay said crossly, leaving the folder on the desk and walking out, really angry at his assumption that she could possibly be interested in re-establishing any sort of liaison outside business hours. Vanity. Charles Rydon was full of it, and how that had escaped her notice during three weeks of seeing him almost every day was as much beyond her as Hugh's belief that she was interested in his cousin. Yet he did think that; every suspicious glare had confirmed it.

CHAPTER SIX

THE secretary gave her a faint smile of recognition. It was their first meeting since Lindsay had stormed into Hugh's office nearly two weeks ago, and because the workshop staff had nothing to do with the administration side of things, she hadn't been up here since.

'Miss . . . Warren, isn't it?' The secretary made out that she had difficulty remembering Lindsay's name. 'Mr Rydon said you were to go straight in.' A slight turn of the head indicated Hugh's door.

Lindsay went over to it, gave a sharp rap and heard Hugh call testily, 'Yes, come in.'

She went in, closed the door, and then stood there just inside the room in a replay of the scene two weeks ago, studying the top of Hugh's dark head as he went on leafing through some papers in front of him. He didn't look up and she didn't say anything.

Then, when he did look up—suddenly—he seemed startled to see her. 'Sorry. I didn't realise you'd come in,' he said brusquely, and, strangely, Lindsay got the impression what he said was true: that his concentration on whatever was on his desk hadn't been feigned like the last time.

'You did want to see me,' she reminded him tartly, aware of a knot of nervousness in the pit of her stomach. It had been one thing to barge into his office in a fury about a stolen opal, another to come as an employee at his bidding, forced to await his convenience, and Lindsay didn't like it—especially not when she found it so difficult to look at him without feeling the burning sensation of his mouth on hers. 'If I'm interrupting . . .' she began uneasily, and broke off as Hugh continued his study of her in silence, in a way that was too intent . . . personal, and yet, conversely, had something dispassionate about it.

Hugh came out of his abstraction with a wave of a hand at the chair by the side of his desk. 'Come and sit down. I won't be a moment.' He picked up the sheaf of papers off his desk and come across the room to the door, disappearing into the secretary's area. Lindsay heard him say something to her—a short snap of an order—before returning empty-handed. 'Sit down,' he said again, and this time Lindsay went over to the chair and perched herself on the edge of it.

Hugh didn't reseat himself behind the desk; he took up a position in front of it, very near her chair—too near. Lindsay was conscious of the faint fragrance of his aftershave, and a tension in the rigid shoulders under the supple, dark material of his jacket. There was an air of nervousness about him too, it seemed to Lindsay as she watched him pick up a small, smooth, stone paperweight off his desk, stare at it and then go through the motion of weighing it up and down in the palm of his hand before closing it up in a tight fist as he suddenly swivelled his eyes to her, cold and grey; mouth taut.

'You and Charles seemed to be getting on very well,' he said tightly through the clamped lips—repressively, as if it was the only way he could hang on to his temper.

Lindsay's first instinct was to let fly, but that was what he was expecting—anger . . . protestations. She held the stony stare for a long moment, then broke into a bright, ingenuous smile. 'Yes, we were, weren't we?' she agreed, ever so pleasantly, and continued the smile without much effort when she saw how much it riled him.

'And just how am I supposed to take that?' Hugh exploded.

Lindsay lifted a shoulder carelessly. 'However you like, Mr Rydon. You made an observation and I simply agreed with it—since it did happen to be true. You saw that for yourself when you came galloping into the workshop to spring us.' Her anger was starting to edge into her voice.

'Don't be absurd,' Hugh snapped, reddening furiously. 'I came to see how you were getting on, that's all. You might remember I wasn't here when you joined us.'

The defensive note didn't escape Lindsay. 'Oh? Is it your normal practice to go down and personally welcome every new employee?' she asked with mock interest and a raised eyebrow.

'That's not the point,' Hugh muttered.

'No, it isn't. You came because Edward happened to tell you that he'd left Charles and me looking through my sketches together—i.e. alone. And that's why you hared down post-haste—to check on us.' Her voice shaking, Lindsay stood up as she spoke. 'If there's nothing else, Mr Rydon . . .'

'Sit down.' Hugh took a step towards her, his body blocking her off, and with nowhere to back, Lindsay sat down again.

They locked glares as he towered over her, looking as if he wanted to inflict grievous bodily harm, and then moved away a few paces into the centre of the room. Lindsay dropped her eyes to the beautiful Persian rug he was standing on, and studied it while she tussled with her temper.

'How do you feel about Charles?'

She lifted her eyes up slowly, gave one swallow and said, with cold contempt, 'Mind your own business, Mr Rydon.'

'It is my business, damn it,' Hugh shot back. 'You seem to have overlooked the fact, not only that my cousin is married, but that he is married to my sister —which makes your interest in him very much my business.'

Lindsay couldn't say what it was about him that made her know Hugh was lying—in part, anyway. He might have been genuinely concerned about the supposed threat to his sister's marriage, but it wasn't the sole reason for his prying. Jealousy. Jealous of Charles? Of Charles' 'relationship' with herself . . . ? She had had the same feeling before and dismissed it as absurd, but now . . .

'Well?' Hugh challenged with a bark.

'Well what, Mr Rydon?' Lindsay countered icily.

'What's going on between you and Charles?'

It was jealousy, Lindsay was almost positive, and it made her want to laugh and tell him 'the love affair of the century' and really give him something to bark about. The man must be barking mad anyway, to imagine she could be continuing the so-called affair with Charles on Ruytons' own premises. What in heaven's name did he think she was? Lindsay knew the answer to that.

'I don't believe you seriously expect me to answer a question like that,' she said frigidly, and stood up again, smoothing her skirt over her thighs, then stopped instantly as Hugh's eyes dropped to follow the hand at her thigh. Idiotically flustered, Lindsay started across the room.

'I haven't finished yet.' The hard, businesslike tone of the voice stopped her at the door in spite of herself. Lindsay turned and waited. 'How have you settled in?' Hugh asked in a surly mutter.

'Very well. Thank you,' she ground out—because she was his employee and the question had been 'business'.

Hugh gave a nod. 'Edwards told me he thinks your designs have possibilities.'

Which was more than Edwards had told her. Lindsay didn't acknowledge the comment. 'Am I dismissed now, Mr Rydon?' she asked stiffly.

'Oh, for God's sake, come off your high horse, Lindsay,' Hugh snarled. 'All right, I admit I had no business asking you about Charles.' He ran a hand irritably through the thick black hair. 'Will you have dinner with me this evening?' he asked in the next breath, quite taking her aback with his nerve . . .

insulting her one moment, asking her out the next.

'No, thank you,' Lindsay declined with frosty primness.

'A drink, then?' Hugh suggested, tempering the angry abruptness with a hurried flash of teeth.

'No, thank you,' she repeated with more ice in her voice, and thought she heard him grind his teeth, but perhaps it was just the working of the jaw that made her think so.

'Why not?' he demanded.

She smiled, dripping acid. 'Because I choose not to. I do have a choice, I suppose? "No strings" I seem to remember. Besides which, I'm already going out for drinks with someone else,' she added and regretted it instantly; she owed Hugh Rydon no explanations for anything.

'Charles,' he growled, predictably and on cue, and Lindsay exploded at last.

'God, you've got a one-track mind, haven't you?' she hurled at him. 'No, it is not Charles. There, does that make you feel better?' She twisted her mouth into a contemptuous smile, 'Your sister can sleep in peace—and you too, Mr Rydon.'

'You certainly don't waste much time spreading your favours around,' Hugh jeered back with a flush she had mistakenly thought was embarrassment, and a smile that was nothing short of a leer.

If she had been closer to him, she would have slapped his face. In blind rage, Lindsay turned on her heel and stormed out of the office and back to the workshop where only Edwards and Philip were still around, the others already having left for the day.

Philip came hurrying up to her as she came charging in, her face thunder. He gave her a quick, curious glance.' There you are, Lindsay, I've been waiting for you—something's come up, I'm afraid. Would you mind terribly if we gave drinks a miss this evening? What about one day next week . . . ?' He watched her face nervously.

'Fine,' Lindsay told him curtly, and headed over to her work-bench to snatch up her coat and bag.

'Listen, Lindsay, are you sure you don't mind?' Philip had followed her and hovered around as she put on the coat. 'You see, I had a telephone call from . . .'

'I don't mind,' Lindsay cut off his explanation with a snap, then, as Philip almost jumped, she forced out an apologetic smile. 'Sorry, Philip, I didn't mean to bite. No, I really don't mind. In fact, I'd prefer to go straight home this evening.'

She let herself out the back way, giving Edwards a quick wave through his glass wall, in no mood to be trapped into one of his circumspect discussions about design philosophy that strained her to death. It was dark outside. Usually, she and Philip left together, taking the short-cut down the two alleys, and Lindsay hadn't realised how much difference it had made having someone—a man—with her on the walk down the dark alley—the width of one car, and with the back walls of the shabby buildings on either side virtually forming a canyon. Her footsteps sounded eerily loud in the silence and she had to keep reminding herself that just around a couple of corners London teemed with frenetic life and in three minutes she would be part of it.

The car turned into the alley somewhere behind her and came cruising down slowly. Lindsay's heart jumped into her mouth as the headlights picked up her hurrying form and threw its gigantic shadow on to the darkened wall ahead. Don't be a fool, it's just someone going home, she told herself, agitated, brushing against the wall to leave every possible distance for the car to pass. And then, when it drew to a halt alongside and the passenger door swung open, cutting off her path forward, Lindsay nearly died of fright.

She came out of her panic-stricken freeze when the driver's door swung open, too. One frantic flick of the eye back towards Ruytons told her it would be madness to try running back; her shortest escape route was forward. Lindsay slammed the passenger door shut and made a bolt for it past the bonnet.

'Lindsay!' Hugh caught her arm at a lunge, yanking her to an abrupt stop.

In the moment of blind panic her eyes refused to recognise him. Lindsay stared wildly and then the recognition, relief and fury all came together. 'You!' she turned on him viciously. 'What the hell do you mean, prowling down the lane after me like that? You scared me to death.' She started to shake violently from the combination of shock and relief.

'Prowling? You thought . . . ?' Hugh suddenly seemed to realise the state she was in, and the next thing Lindsay knew, she was wrapped tightly in his arms, just being held. 'It's OK, you're all right now,' he murmured soothingly. 'And, honestly, I didn't mean to frighten you. But you shouldn't have been walking down here alone, it might just as easily not have been me.'

Lindsay pulled her face away from the comforting shoulder and tore herself out of Hugh's arms. 'The main street is just around the corner,' she muttered, embarrassed to have needed comforting out of her fright like a child, and on the defensive because it had been a stupid thing to be in the alley by herself. 'And I don't appreciate being followed.'

'Talk about paranoia.' Hugh laughed, unamused. 'I was not following you. Taylor had left the car for me at the back of Ruytons, and I was simply on my way home,' he explained with strained patience. 'Now, where do you want me to drop you off for this date of yours?'

'I haven't got a date. That is, I . . .' Lindsay began to explain and changed her mind. 'I was on my way home,' she muttered reluctantly.

'Well, get in anyway, and I'll run you home,' Hugh ordered, after the slight pause it took him to work out that either she'd lied to him about the date in the first place, or had been shamed into changing her mind about it. 'Still at that hotel place?'

'Yes,' Lindsay said, and allowed herself to be handed into the car without argument, because after her fright she wasn't up to tackling the dark alley, and Hugh would not have driven off and left her anyway.

'How about that drink, then?' he suggested when he was behind the wheel again. 'Look, Lindsay, I really did want to talk to you,' he went on, throwing her a quick, oblique glance. 'To apologise. For pretty much everything . . . Damn.' Hugh broke off as the downpour descended from nowhere, instantly obliterating the sinister shapes of the alley. He flicked on the windscreen wipers and concentrated on manoeuvring the large car around the tight corner into the lane which brought them out into the blare and flare of the busy street.

'Where are you taking me?' Lindsay asked sharply when Hugh turned left instead of right to head towards her hotel in Bayswater.

'A place I know . . .' he told her offhandedly. For a drink. And a quiet talk. And please don't jump down my throat and say you won't come,' he added with a wry weariness that surprised Lindsay into giving him a concerned look. 'I'm not up to arguing tonight, and that's all we ever seem to do, isn't it? Argue and trade insults.'

True, Lindsay thought, and whose fault is that? She didn't say it, but the snide question must have beamed itself from her mind.

'Yes, my fault, I know,' Hugh conceded drily. 'And I do apologise—for my behaviour at our first meeting; my reasons were no excuse. And for coming on so crassly after our dinner last week, and as for prying about Charles . . .'

Lindsay listened in astonished, suspicious silence, not sure she was hearing right.

'It was unforgivable, and I'm sorry. It won't happen again, I promise. So how about a truce?' Hugh finished abruptly.

The question hung between them as they drove

through the rain and heavy traffic along the river before Hugh turned up into a side-street and then another. The traffic was a barely distinguishable buzz in the rain when they stopped in a quiet street of imposing-looking houses facing a small square.

Hugh turned off the ignition. 'Truce, Lindsay?' he asked again.

Lindsay turned to him and gave a small shrug, which he took for assent and smiled at her, looking suddenly boyish. 'Where are we?' she asked, since they appeared to have arrived somewhere.

'My place, I want to drop off my suitcase and a few other bits and change my clothes before we go on. Do you mind?' Hugh explained, not giving her time to react.

'Oh. No . . . no, that's all right, 'Lindsay answered, a little nonplussed as it dawned on her that Hugh must have come straight into the office on his return from his business trip. She felt a twinge of guilt, too, for having jumped to the instant conclusion that he'd brought her to his place for anything less innocent.

They dashed into the house through the rain, laughing like a pair of children as they caught their breath and brushed the rain off their coats in the hall—blissfully warm, with an overall warmth that came from continuous central heating and thick carpets, not a stingy two-bar radiator and tatty rugs.

Hugh dropped his suitcase on to the floor and opened a door off the hall. 'Come into the sitting-room, it'll be warmer for you,' he invited, shepherd-ind her in. 'The housekeeper won't be back from her week off until tomorrow morning, so I'm afraid the fire isn't on. I'll light it in a minute, but first I want to nip upstairs and change. I feel I've been in this wretched suit for days—I have, actually. Travelling light does have a few drawbacks, 'Hugh grinned ruefully. 'Make yourself at home. I won't be long.'

The room was a surprise—a very comfortable sitting-room rather than the elegant drawing-room Ruytons' ultra-elegant environment would have led her to expect. It had a very lived-in look about it, but something seemed to be missing. Lindsay wandered about, faintly puzzled, and then it struck her—the something missing was a feminine atmosphere. It struck her, too, that what she had been looking out for were signs of a woman's presence . . . little giveaway things like bowls of pot-pourri, a pretty tapestry. Pure feminine curiosity, and Lindsay was annoyed with herself for succumbing to it, and for going on to wonder what sort of relationship Hugh had with . . . whoever. Obviously there had to be someone in his life, because men like Hugh Rydon didn't get to be—what? Thirty-five . . . thirty-six?—without an attachment somewhere. An accommodating attachment it had to be too, if the way he felt free to ask other women to dinner, and into his house, was any indication. Not an arrangement Lindsay would have cared for herself. She would want to be the only woman in her man's life . . . would want commitment, fidelity. Marriage. Laughingly old-fashioned, perhaps, and Charles had teasingly called her that when he'd realised he couldn't charm her into bed after their first couple of of dates. All the more ironic, that Hugh could believe her promiscuous when she was in fact as strait-laced as the proverbial maiden aunt.

'Well, what would you like to do?' Hugh asked, coming into the room casually dressed in navy trousers and a camel-coloured polo-necked sweater, and looking an entirely different person out of his 'uniform'. 'What about a drink while you decide?' he suggested, going to the lovely corner cabinet and opening it to reveal a selection of bottles. 'Or would you prefer coffee?'

Her better judgement warned her to refuse either and tell him she would prefer to go to a pub—somewhere jangling with noise and people all around. 'Safer' was the word that sprang to Lindsay's mind. 'A vermouth, if you have it,' she replied, disregarding the warning in her head with a mental shrug. And, several hours later, she could not have reconstructed the sequel of events which had led to her sitting in front of a blazing fire, sipping liqueur and coffee after the meal Hugh had had delivered from 'the little place around the corner' which, if the delicious veal casserole was any guide, had to be run by a cordon bleu cook.

Lindsay felt very relaxed, mellow almost, and could not have said how—when that had come about, either. Some time between the first drink and Hugh's suggestion to have a meal delivered, her tension had melted away, and while the bottle of excellent wine with the meal had undoubtedly contributed, it hadn't been entirely responsible for the enjoyable evening and the conversation that just seemed to flow.

Music; films; books . . . travel—all carefully
neutral topics, but none the less it had been fun to
discuss them with someone who turned out to share a
lot of her tastes.

'Has Charles spoken to you about the exhibition?'
Hugh asked, looking up at her from the floor where
he was propped up on an elbow, his long, lean body
stretched out on the rug in front of the fire.

The charge of tension shot through her at the
mention of Charles' name. Was the truce over
already, and Hugh about to spoil the pleasant
evening with yet another interminable dissection of
her 'relationship' with his cousin? 'No,' Lindsay
replied flatly, keeping the edge out of her voice. 'I
haven't yet even been officially told when it's to be.'

'Nor me,' Hugh tossed in with a laugh. 'I'm not at
all up in these extra-curricular activities, thank
heavens, but I gather it's in a fortnight or so, and
with a bit of luck I should still be away. I'm due to fly
off to New York about a week before it and won't
dare to come back until it's over. The place goes
positively haywire. You'll see,' he warned, smiling.

'Don't you ever go to any of "these extra-
curricular activities"?' Lindsay asked, curious about
the division of activity between him and Charles—a
natural division when she thought about. She tried to
imagine Hugh flapping about organising the models,
selecting the jewellery, flattering socialities, and
couldn't—any more than she could picture Charles
working on projection of annual turnover or
negotiating terms of trade with suppliers. The cousins

were chalk and cheese.

'Not if I can help it,' Hugh assured her with a mock shudder. 'To each his own, and all that. Now tell me about your plans,' he switched subject abruptly. 'What are you thinking of doing about long-term accommodation? You're not planning to stay on in that place indefinitely, are you?'

' "That place", as you call it, happens to be all I can afford for the moment,' said Lindsay defensively, over-reacting to Hugh's dismissive description. 'I know it's not much more than a boarding house, but it isn't all that bad, and . . .'

'I wasn't implying that it was,' Hugh broke in with an angry laugh. 'Honestly, Lindsay, I didn't mean to sound critical; it's just that I never know what to call those places. They're not really hotels as such, are they?'

'No, or I couldn't afford to be staying in one for so long.' Lindsay pulled her horns in, realising just how very tenuous their truce was if she could take exception to a perfectly innocent comment about Mrs Layton's awful place. 'Anyway, I shan't be there much longer. Kelly and I are hoping to move out soon and get a flat together,' she volunteered to make up for her burst of snideness.

'Are you?' Hugh sounded really interested. 'Your friend is a very stunning-looking lady,' he added, as any man would have, and a sudden glow which wasn't from the fire came into his eyes; to her own amazement, Lindsay felt a stir of something she recognised as plain, old-fashioned jealousy. Jealous that Hugh thought Kelly stunning?

'Yes, she's absolutely gorgeous, isn't she?' She overdid the enthusiasm a little wildly; idiotic, when she really did think Kelly gorgeous. 'She's set her sights on being a top model, and is bound to make it very soon, I think.' Some peculiar compulsion made Lindsay want to keep Kelly the topic of conversation.

'*Fait accompli,* with a face and personality like that,' Hugh agreed, guilelessly, and gave Lindsay's curious jealousy an unwitting nudge. Or was it deliberate? Lindsay looked away, flustered, from Hugh's amused gaze. 'Anyway, let me know when you plan to start flat-hunting and I'll drive you around—both of you,' he offered, with a suspicion of a twinkle, then eased himself to his feet and went over to the far side of the room to put on another tape.

'Thank you,' Lindsay said politely, and watched him fiddle with the cassette player, knowing that she would never be taking him up on his offer because, however sincere Hugh was at this moment, it would be a different story tomorrow . . . next week, when this strangely companionable interlude was over and they were back to their tension-ridden roles of employer and employee. And you didn't just walk into the boss's office and say, 'About your offer to help me flat-hunt,' as you would to a friend, or lover. Hugh was neither—nor likely to be; one pleasant evening didn't make a friendship, and Lindsay doubted any woman could have a friendship—a platonic one—with Hugh Rydon.

As she watched him across the room, some of her earlier tension began to flicker into uneasy life, heightening as Hugh came back to the fireplace and settled himself down on the floor again, only this time beside her armchair, with his back and shoulders resting against the front edge of its arm. No part of him was touching her, yet he might as well have had his head in her lap for all the difference it would have made. Lindsay went as rigid as a rock, while Hugh seemed totally unconscious of the effect his nearness was having on her. He leant back and closed his eyes, listening to the poignant strains of the music.

On guard, Lindsay stared into the mass of springy black waves within hand's reached, waiting for a move from Hugh . . . the ever-so-casual hand happening to find itself on her knee, or something equally predictable. And then she appalled herself with her own insane urge to run her fingers through the black hair.

Was that what Hugh was waiting for—a move from her? Was this a set-up, after all? He had as good as told her he wouldn't be forcing himself on her again, but that didn't mean he didn't intend to manipulate the situation in such a way that it would be the most natural thing in the world to find herself in his arms.

And how much more subtly manipulative could you get? Head almost in her lap, soft, romantic music, a fire in the grate; even the lights had been turned off so they could enjoy the fire better. Talk about transparent. Lindsay kept her hand firmly in her lap.

The music had stopped some moments ago, but another sound continued to break the warm silence of the room, and it took Lindsay a long, puzzled moment before she associated the steady, rhythmic sound with Hugh, and then she had trouble believing it. Hugh was asleep—very definitely, and very fast, asleep. She stared down at him in a mixture of surprise and amusement before the amusement took over and she had to restrain herself from laughing aloud—at herself.

There she had sat, convinced it was all a ploy, expecting at any moment Hugh to come lazily to life and make the pass she felt the whole evening had been leading up to, while all the time, Hugh was simply drifting off to sleep.

Hugh made a small, indrawn sound. A snore. Faint, but unmistakably a snore. Lindsay stifled a giggle, and, taking care not to disturb him, eased herself out of the armchair, then stood looking down at him, wondering how she could ever have thought Hugh Rydon intimidating, or in any way threatening. He looked about as threatening as a child, and with the same air of vulnerability that children had in their sleep.

What was this man all about? Arrogant, rude . . . warm, pleasant. Attractive. In other circumstances they might have liked each other instead of just being attracted to each other in spite of themselves—a physical, chemical—sexual—attraction, nothing more. Yet perhaps it could be, Lindsay thought with a strange sense of yearning that she found unsettling. She turned away and hurried softly over to the big chesterfield to gather up her coat and bag, and sneaked out of the room.

She was the first one into the workshop the next morning—aside from Edwards, whom Lindsay half suspected of never going home. She had never met anyone so single-minded about his job . . . more than a job, a way of life; and it made Lindsay stop and rethink her own goals. She wanted to be the best, but at what price?

'Telephone, Lindsay.' Edwards beckoned her into his office as Lindsay came out from the little kitchen at the end of the workshop where staff made themselves tea or coffee throughout the day, and discreetly wandered out as Lindsay picked up the receiver, giving herself one guess as to who would be on the other end of the line. She wasn't wrong.

'Hello?' she said, and felt the familiar tingle down her spine at the low, husky voice in her ear.

'Lindsay—Hugh. I heard you came in early. About last night . . .' Hugh launched straight into his apology. 'What can I say? I'm most awfully sorry.'

Lindsay gave a small chuckle. 'That's OK, forget it,' she told him lightly.

'Forget it? How can I?' Hugh groaned. 'It was abominably rude of me, and I can't think how it could happened.'

'That's easy. You were tired,' Lindsay pointed out with a smile in her voice.

'You can say that again, but that's no excuse. Did you get home all right?' he asked, concerned.

'Yes, of course I did. I telephoned for a cab from your hall. I didn't walk,' she assured him, laughing.

'You should have wakened me,' Hugh admonished in a mock growl. 'Will you come out with me on

Sunday?' he slipped in deftly. 'Let me make up for my appalling manners . . .'

There was a long silence while Lindsay hesitated, wanting to say 'yes', yet curiously nervous of doing it.

'I thought you might be interested in a drive down to a pub in Surrey where they have a really great little jazz group on. You told me you like jazz, and you'll love these guys. And I promise not to fall asleep.' Hugh's hurried 'sale' of the date made him come over like an anxious teenager. 'Say yes, Lindsay,' he ordered with an appeal edging through his voice.

'Yes,' said Lindsay quickly, looking through the glass wall at Edwards talking to Philip who had just come in.

'Good.' Hugh gave a little laugh—of relief, it seemed to Lindsay. 'I'll pick you up at your hotel at eleven-thirty. Does that suit you?'

'Yes. Thank you,' Lindsay murmured. 'Look, Hugh, I'd better go now,' she added as Edwards finished with Philip and came to hover near his office, trying not to hover too close.

'Right. See you around,' Hugh said cheerfully.

'Yes,' Lindsay said, but didn't see him the whole day, and was only aware at the end of it that she was disappointed Hugh hadn't come by. Which was silly, because she knew he rarely came down to the workshop. And why should he come especially to see her? Because, never mind what he thought about her and Charles, Hugh was interested in her, she was sure of it, and the realisation gave her a surprising amount of pleasure.

CHAPTER SEVEN

AT FIRST Lindsay was disappointed that the pub was not out in the country as she had expected, but the winding neighbourhood high street had a very villagey look and feel about it, with lots of quaint little shops interspersed among the mandatory chain supermarkets and eating houses, and she insisted on stopping and peering into each one as she and Hugh strolled along on their way to the pub.

It had turned out sunny, if not actually warm, and the change from three weeks of unremitting greyness made her spirits soar and gave her a very good idea why sun-starved English holidaymakers packed themselves off in droves to the resorts of the Mediterranean coastline. Lindsay felt she had shed the weight of the world off her shoulders without the heavy, navy coat, which she had replaced with a lighter tweedy jacket over dark slacks and cream sweater. Her hair was loose about her face; the bruising had long disappeared, but she discovered she liked the softer style, although today it meant constantly flicking wind-blown strands off her face.

She was aware of Hugh glancing at her as they walked slowly towards the pub, her arm com-

panionably through his. That had happened just
after getting out of the car, when Hugh had simply
taken her hand and slipped it through his arm, and
after the first few moments of self-consciousness
Lindsay didn't give it a second thought. It seemed
natural—a part of the something new and nice that
had established itself between them since the
evening at Hugh's house. Perhaps it was falling
asleep that had taken the final edge off the tension
between them. They could laugh about it—and
did, with Hugh going on so much about it when he
picked her up outside the hotel, and on the drive,
that in the end Lindsay had threatened to scream if
he apologised one more time.

She intercepted one of Hugh's glances as she was
flicking the hair off her face yet again. 'Why do
you keep looking at me like that?' she asked, more
intrigued than anything else.

'Because you're so very beautiful with the
sunlight dancing off your hair and out of your
eyes. They're like sapphires, did you know that?'
The warm admiration in his eyes brought a sudden
warm glow to her face.

Wild flattery, and Lindsay loved every word of
it. 'Then you do know your gems, after all,' she
quipped, and it was a measure of her new relaxed
mood that she hadn't seized up with embarrassment or suspicion as she would have if Hugh had
come out with something as outrageous a week
ago.

'I take it you've heard stories to the contrary?
I've heard them myself,' he admitted with a wry

laugh. 'There is something different about you today, though, Lindsay.' His eyes ranged intently over her face. 'You're positively glowing.'

'Thank you,' Lindsay murmured, colouring more and feeling strangely shy, and thinking she wasn't the only one who seemed different today. Or was it that they were simply letting their real selves show through for once? She certainly felt more the person she had been when she left Sydney than the shrewish, biting stranger who had turned up in a shabby hotel in Bayswater.

The pub was an old building, lying charmingly in the curve of the river, and the jazz belted out at them as they approached, half deafening them before they had reached the door, and then nearly finishing the job when they walked in to the finale of 'When The Saints Come Marching In'.

'Our song?' mouthed Hugh into her ear as an enormous burly man, standing to the front of the band, roared out the words in a voice so gravelly it could have been spread over a road.

Lindsay giggled.

It hadn't occurred to her that Hugh had brought her to a regular haunt of his until the break that followed, when he took her around from table to table and introduced her to so many people that she didn't have a hope of remembering names. He finished off by introducing her to the members of the band, whose gravel-voiced singer, Gerry, turned out to be an old friend of Hugh's.

Lindsay didn't know why she should have felt so surprised—why she had assumed Hugh's friends had

to be smart-looking, sophisticated businessmen—
with elegant female counterparts.

'From Australia? Sydney, is it?' Gerry beamed
some awful nicotine-stained teeth at her through
the untidy gingery-grey beard. 'Took the band over
there once. Years ago—long before you were born,
luv.' He roared with laughter and sent his enormous bulk quivering. 'Delighted to meet you,
Lindsay; look after her now, Hughie,' he ordered
giving her another beam before wandering off, and
'Hughie' put an arm around her shoulder, which
Lindsay found she didn't mind at all.

They stayed until the pub closed at two-thirty,
drinking some beer, listening to traditional old
favourites, and chatting in between, and only when
the session wound up did Lindsay realise the afternoon had a long way to go with lunch on the
agenda at the house of a couple who had been at
their table. Elaine and Bill somebody . . . Lindsay
couldn't remember their surname.

'Are you sure Elaine won't mind me coming
along too?' Lindsay asked, concerned for the poor
hostess who was about to have half the pub
descending on her for Sunday lunch.

'Good grief no,' Hugh assured her. 'She'd be
terribly miffed if you didn't come. I rather suspect
she counts heads to make sure no one has escaped
when it's her turn to put on the lunch. She loves
doing it—they all do. We—they,' Hugh amended
quickly, 'take it in turns to feed the mob; the rest
of us bring along something—apart from our
appetites, that is.'

And when they returned to the car, Lindsay noticed the several patisserie boxes and a package that had to be a couple of bottles of wine in the back seat.

So this was what Hugh did on Sunday afternoons. Today with her . . . but what about other Sundays? Lindsay was none the wiser as the afternoon wore on. There were about a dozen and a half people milling about, serving themselves roast beef and all the trimmings from the sideboard, and talking furiously all the time above the tape of still more jazz, but no one seemed particularly surprised or curious that Hugh had brought her along, and no one asked him—at least not in Lindsay's presence—about any Jill or Sue or Liz. But then, of coure, they wouldn't. You didn't ask after other girlfriends in the presence of the latest.

Latest? Girlfriend? Was that what she thought she was? Lindsay stopped the disconcerting thought in its tracks, embarrassed when she caught Hugh's eye through a space in the wall of bodies that separated them from each other. She returned her attention hurriedly to Gerry, who seemed to had adopted her for the afternoon. She was sitting on the sofa with him, squeezed into one corner, Gerry squeezed into the rest of it, while he told her the story of how he had taken his band to Australia for some jazz convention about thirty years ago. 'Years before you were born, luv,' he reminded her again, and seemed to enjoy the fact that he was old enough to be her father. 'Hello, Hughie.' He

suddenly grinned up at Hugh who had come over to
their corner. 'Come to rescue your lovely lady from
my clutches? Not before time. I've been boring the
. . . er . . . socks off you, haven't I, luv? You're safe
now, though. I'm going, and Hughie is staying.'
Gerry bellowed a laugh and hauled his massive frame
up off the sofa. 'Make sure you bring her along again
real soon,' he instructed Hugh facetiously, but for
the first time Lindsay saw something like curiosity in
those pale eyes as they flicked from her to Hugh and
back to her again. He gave Lindsay's hand an
excruciating squeeze of farewell, and Hugh a thump
on the shoulder that made Lindsay flinch for him.

'I might just do that,' laughed Hugh in reply, but
looking at Lindsay. 'What do you think? he asked
softly as Gerry ambled away.

Lindsay nodded, hoping he would ask her again,
but uncertain as to whether he would . . . whether she
had simply taken some other woman's place for the
day—a lovely day. And she was sorry when it was
over.

'I've had a lovely time. Thank you,' she said
sincerely when they drew up in front of the familiar,
shabby façade of her hotel. 'You won't mind if I
don't ask you up? I . . .' Lindsay broke off, unable
to put into words that she didn't want their day to
end in a small, cold room with nowhere to sit
comfortably, and lukewarm instant coffee from
chipped mugs.

'No, I don't mind,' Hugh's smile reassured her he
meant what he said. 'Thank you for coming with me
today,' he said, so formally that for an instant

Lindsay expected him to shake hands.

'Thank you for asking me,' she replied, formally too, and then they just looked at each other. The next step should have been a kiss, but Hugh didn't take it, and Lindsay felt the disappointment as a sudden swift tightening in her chest. 'Well, good-night, then,' she said quickly, forgetting that, dark as it was, five-thirty in the afternoon wasn't exactly the night. She turned to reach for the door-handle.

'Lindsay . . .'

The tone of Hugh's voice made her heart skip a beat. Lindsay took her hand away from the door and turned her head around slowly.

'Please don't tense up like that,' Hugh said, placing his hand over hers as they clutched the bag on her lap. 'I promised you I would never force myself on you again.'

How much force had he used to elicit her response last time? None that Lindsay could remember, and he certainly didn't need to use any now. She wanted him to kiss her, surely he could tell that? Lindsay's lips parted in mute appeal, her eyes carrying the same message as they stayed fixed on Hugh's mouth, watching it draw closer, and in the final moment before their lips touched it was she who put her hands to his face, cupping it as she surrendered herself to the long, sweet kiss that seemed to leave a warm imprint on her mouth for hours after Hugh had driven away.

She was on a high all during the following week, immune to the return of sunless grey skies, happy and distracted, and barely able to concentrate on

anything but the next date with Hugh—theatre and
supper the next Saturday night; too far away for
Lindsay, but Hugh had said he would be busy during
the week, and she was so elated that he was asking
her out again, that it didn't cross her mind to wonder
what was going to keep him so busy.

Madness; sheer, utter insanity to be whirling about
like an infatuated schoolgirl and laying herself open
to everybody's amused curiosity. 'Have you won the
Pools, Lindsay?'—that from all the chaps in the
workshop, except Edwards, who confined himself to
the odd intent stare.

'Been at the champagne, darling?'—from Charles,
and 'Lindsay, you're in love!' predictably from
Kelly, who must have been born with a guarantee to
jump to a wrong conclusion if there was one around,
thought Lindsay, fending off her friend's curiosity
with a laugh during one of their intermittent meals
together at the café near the hotel, and changing the
subject—easily done with Kelly being uncharacteristi-
cally down in the dumps and only too eager to talk
endlessly about what rotters clients were when they
took forever to decide who they wanted for their
campaigns.

'They never think of anybody but themselves,'
Kelly growled at least a dozen times during each
meal, and it was no use Lindsay trying to tell her it
was the client's money, after all, and that these things
took time; Kelly knew that perfectly well herself, but
refused to be cheered, wallowing in thinking the
worst . . . that the client wasn't going to want her
anyway . . . that she was washed up as a model . . .

It was out of sheer glazed-eyed desperation that Lindsay suddenly thought to mention the coming exhibition and the fact that Ruytons would be needing models for their pieces.

Kelly's transformation was instantaneous. 'Oh, Lindsay, please, please, please ask them,' she begged effusively, eyes a hundred watts brighter. 'I'll be ever so sophisticated, or superior—or whatever they want me to be, only please, please ask whoever is in charge of the show if they would consider me? It's not Hugh, is it?'

'No. Charles—his cousin.'

'Do you know him, too?'

'Yes,' Lindsay admitted shortly, and almost regretted her own impulsive suggestion when she realised it meant asking a favour of Charles.

Charles had been getting very much on her nerves lately, turning up in her work area too often by far, always starting off the session on some design matter, but never failing to end with trying to persuade her into going out with him: to dinner, drinks. Only the persuasion was beginning to smack suspiciously of pestering, and Lindsay didn't like it. But she asked him anyway, because she had promised, and because Kelly would never have forgiven her if she hadn't.

Charles made out that he was thinking deeply. 'Well, then,' he said after a long moment of furrowing his brow, 'what say I call by on Saturday evening and take you and this stunning friend of yours out for a drink so we can all talk about it?' he suggested. 'Darling, I'm sure she's every bit as super as you say, but I do need to see her for myself, you know,' he pointed out, a little peevishly, as Lindsay's face showed what she thought of his suggestion. And she hated the 'darlings' that he kept slipping in with teeth-grinding regularity.

'I know that, Charles.' Lindsay tried to restrain her irritation. 'But Saturday night is out. I have no idea what Kelly's plans are, but I'm going out myself and being picked up at seven-thirty, so Saturday is just not on,' she explained, and then regretted it when she saw Charles' eyes sharpen with interest at the mention of her going out. 'What about this evening after work . . . ?' she suggested, in her turn. 'I could telephone Kelly and . . .'

'No good.' Charles was shaking his head, very regretfully. 'I have a standing engagement on Thursday nights.'

With his own wife, she shouldn't wonder. 'Some time next week, then,' Lindsay said crossly, wishing she had never mentioned Kelly to him at all—nor the exhibition to Kelly.

Charles settled himself on the edge of her work-bench and looked as if he had nothing else to do but resolve their dilemma. 'Tell you what: I'll call by at your place on Saturday afternoon instead and . . .'

'I'll need to check with Kelly,' Lindsay interrupted hurriedly, trying to think of something that wouldn't bring him near the hotel.

'Shouldn't bother,' Charles dismissed her objection with an airy wave of his slim hand. 'If she's not in I'll just go away and we can make it another day. So I'll come by around five and we can nip out for a quick drink, which will give you plenty of time to get back and make yourself pretty for that important date of yours.' His mouth was smiling but his eyes were not; they held a faintly malicious gleam in them, which made her wonder if he'd guessed she was going out with Hugh. 'Now, what's the address of that place you're staying at?' Charles whipped out a notebook from nowhere, picked up a pen off her bench and waited expectantly.

Lindsay had no choice but to give it to him, cursing herself for having walked into his neatly laid trap. The last thing she wanted was Charles knowing where she lived and feeling free to 'drop by' to make a nuisance of himself. Oh, bother him, she thought later; he could just as easily have ferreted out her address from Mrs Buchanan's records if he hadn't already, so what did it matter? And it was Kelly he wanted to see, anyway—she hoped, not entirely convinced. She determined to be as cool and off-putting as she possible could without jeopardising Kelly's chances of the job. Lindsay would not have put it past him to veto Kelly if he felt himself slighted—or something. There was a very definite streak of malice in Charles Rydon, she decided, and only wondered that it had taken her so long to realise it.

And then, on Saturday afternoon when he didn't show up, Lindsay didn't know what he was playing at. Five o'clock had come and gone, and she and Kelly were still sitting about in the foyer, Kelly's excited anticipation fizzling like air from a pricked balloon as five-thirty became five forty-five, and then six.

'That's it, he's forgotten. Not interested,' Kelly pronounced gloomily. 'Come on back upstairs, Lindsay, I'm sick of hanging around here. And I think he's jolly rude for standing us up like this.'

Lindsay could not have agreed more, but she was relieved, too. 'There's probably some explanation,'she said, lamely, not able to think of anything.

'Yes, he's not interested,' muttered Kelly crossly. 'Oh, well, plenty more fish in the sea and all that, but it would have been super to be able to include Ruytons in my file,' she added wistfully as they trailed up the interminable flights of stairs to their landing.

Kelly was due to go out, too, but Lindsay took first turn in the bathroom because she was being picked up earlier, and she was dressed and putting the final touches to her make-up when the footsteps sounded on the stairs—too heavy for any of the other female occupants of the floor. Very definitely masculine.

Hugh, already? She glanced nervously at her watch. Seven-fifteen. Surprised, Lindsay grabbed her coat and handbag and was moving to the door when the rap sounded—sharp . . . impatient. She opened the door on a little surge of annoyance—to Charles whistling wheezily under his breath.

'Hello, darling,' he greeted her with his by-now standard familiarity, and then took a step back and stared at her. 'Do you know, I'd actually forgotten how fabulous you can look.'

Lindsay thought she looked pretty good too, in

the dark sapphire 1930s-looking two piece wool jersey dress, but was not interested in a confirmation from Charles. 'What are you doing here?' She jerked herself out of her angry surprise.

'I've come to meet your friend, remember . . . ? Sorry I'm a bit late and all that. No chance of drinks now, I suppose?' Charles had the hide to grin into Lindsay's frozen face, then spun round as a door slammed at the end of the corridor, and Lindsay too stuck her head out the door to see Kelly come gliding towards them in a crimson, madly patterned kimono.

Kelly was gorgeous at any time, but straight out of a bath, skin glowing, she looked too lovely to be true. Charles couldn't take his eyes off her as she glided up to them and looked at Lindsay questioningly.

'You must be Kelly. I'm Charles.' Charles focused the full beam of his best, most charming smile on Kelly, and Kelly returned one with just as much force, and it was hard to say which of them was more captivated by the other.

Lindsay tossed up whether to just leave them to admire each other. She hovered irritably in the doorway while Charles began what she recognised immediately as his patter. 'Look,' she said testily after a few moments of listening to the nonsense, 'you two stay and get to know each other; I must dash.' She simply closed her door and left them. Let Kelly get rid of Charles when she chose—if she chose; all Lindsay wanted was to get down the stairs and out of the hotel—alone, to wait for

Hugh—out on the footpath if need be; anywhere that was away from Charles. There was a panic welling up inside her that Hugh might see her with Charles and think the worst—resume thinking the worst about her; and just when they were beginning to know and like each other.

He mustn't see her with Charles; not her in her hotel, was Lindsay's one frantic thought as she flew down the stairs, and had reached the bottom of the last flight when Charles came pelting down behind her.

'I thought you wanted to talk to Kelly,' she hissed, throwing an agitated glance across the foyer to the glass doors of the entrance.

'Oh, we've arranged to meet again early next week,' Charles told her cheerfully, and must have arranged it in about thirty seconds flat—fast, even by Charles' standards. 'She really is a stunner, isn't she?'

'Isn't she?' returned Lindsay over her shoulder as she set off in a rush across the foyer, Charles breathing down her neck.

Half-way across, he suddenly made a grab at her arm and pulled her to a stop. 'I say, Lindsay, I'm truly very sorry about turning up so late. I know you're angry—and look very beautiful with it.' He smiled maddeningly, and Lindsay would have given anything to hit him.

The angry, grating laugh burst out of her, a note of hysteria in it, but the sound of her anger would not have reached Hugh. Lindsay saw him come in through the glass doors and saw instantly what he was seeing: her laughing face, Charles smiling at her, his hand intimately on her arm. She met Hugh's eye and blanched, and even from the distance that separated them, she must have presented a picture of guilt. Hugh's face turned into a deadly stony mask in front of her eyes, and Lindsay felt sick.

'What's . . . ?' Charles swung his head in the direction of her white-faced stare and broke into a rueful, embarrassed grin—for his cousin's benefit. 'Your date, I presume?' he murmured softly, purring malice, and keeping his hand on her arm.

Lindsay dislodged it in a furious upward jerk as Hugh started towards them, looking through both of them.

'Hello, Hugh, old chap. This is a surprise.' Charles kept up the grinning and managed to look sly and confused at the same time. 'I just popped by for a few moments, didn't I, Lindsay?' he explained earnestly, and made the truth sound like a lie. 'Well, I'll be off . . .' he said with jangling brightness when the silence threatened to go on for ever, and with another nervous-looking grin he ambled towards the door, whistling nonchalantly under his breath.

He had done it deliberately: put on his show of surprise and guilt and all that awful embarrassment at having been 'sprung' by Hugh. He'd turned up late, probably with the sole intention of being around when Hugh came to call for her. And she had thought Hugh was jealous of Charles? The boot seemed well and truly on the other foot, and,

incredibly, it was Charles who was acting as if
Hugh was edging him out. Out of what? There had
never been anything for him to be edged out of.
But Hugh didn't know that.

Lindsay forced herself to look into Hugh's face
and saw that Charles' mean, award-winning performance had had as much success as he could
have ever wished.

'Hello, Lindsay. Are you ready?' Hugh
enquired, courteously, ice in his voice—and eyes;
they held the same distancing distaste she had seen
in them on their first meeting when he had assumed
all those dreadful things about her.

Lindsay nodded dumbly.

'Shall we go?' he suggested, gesturing towards
the door, and Lindsay was searingly conscious of
the distance Hugh was keeping between them as
they walked in silence across the foyer.

'Have a pleasant evening,' muttered Mr Layton
lugubriously from behind the reception desk, and
sounded as if he was wishing a plague upon them.

Outside, Hugh kept the same deliberate distance,
omitting even the perfunctory hand at the elbow to
guide her down the steps. Lindsay felt embarrassed
and angry at the calculated slight.

'Look, if you'd prefer to call the evening off, I
. . . ' she faltered.

'No. Why should I?' Hugh asked blandly. 'I've
been looking forward to our evening together very
much,' he told her in what might have been a
courteous afterthought, but which Lindsay knew
was meant to hurt.

She, too, had been looking forward to it, damn it—right up until Charles had turned up to put his foot in it. Now she couldn't think of anything more horrible than the prospect of the unbearably long, tense hours in Hugh's company, knowing he wished himself anywhere but with her. Why hadn't he just turned around and walked out when he saw her and Charles together? Good manners? Spite, more like—to make her feel as rotten as he could.

There was no question of trying to explain that Charles had called by to meet Kelly . . . that she was almost at the point of not being able to stand him, and that there'd never been an affair. Hugh would have taken every word for guilty self-justification, and not believed her if her life depended on it.

If only she had explained everything last Sunday; that would have been the right time to put the misunderstanding about the supposed affair behind them once and for all. But Lindsay had believed then that it was behind them, that somewhere along the line Hugh had already realised he had misjudged her.

'Here we are.' Hugh stopped beside his car and unlocked the passenger side-door. He held it open for her, and again it was humiliatingly obvious that he was going out of his way not to touch her. Lindsay climbed in and he shut the door—no handing her into the car as he had done every previous occasion.

I'm not a leper and I haven't just been to bed with Charles, she wanted to cry out when Hugh got in beside her. Rigid with anger and mortification, Lindsay bit hard into her bottom lip to stop herself from raging at him. How dared he make his facile assumptions about her? How could he?

She stayed silent, but Hugh chatted as he drove.

With an icy civility he commented on reviews of the show they were about to see, the weather clearing up, the increase of traffic in the city; it was a parody of the polite date, and Lindsay thought she would go mad listening to him.

'It seems to be clearing to a fine night,' Hugh said; he had already said that earlier—and would probably say it again.

Lindsay clenched her teeth, perilously close to tears, which she had to blink back furiously. She wouldn't—couldn't cry in front of this cold, cruelly courteous stranger.

'I did not have an affair with Charles in Sydney, and I'm not having one with him now.' She hadn't said that? Surely that defensive, pathetic mumble hadn't come out of her mouth? Lindsay froze, holding her breath, and sensed Hugh suddenly turn his eyes to her.

CHAPTER EIGHT

'WHAT did you say?' Hugh's cold, formal stranger act dissolved in a harsh hiss.

Lindsay wouldn't look at him and could not have repeated what she'd unconsciously let slip, because if she opened her mouth again it would only have been to howl.

She heard Hugh mutter an obscenity, and then the next moment he screeched the car into a sharp left turn in the path of an oncoming car, getting an angry hoot of the horn for his reckless manoeuvre.

He could have rammed them headlong into a bus for all Lindsay cared. She stared tearily ahead, not taking any notice of anything, and it wasn't until Hugh drew up outside his house that she realised he hadn't been driving them to the theatre.

'I want to go home,' she protested angrily when Hugh stormed over to her side, flung the door open and pulled her out of the seat. And then they had an undignified tussle right there on the footpath as she struggled to get herself out of his grip, hitting at him with her free hand and not getting anywhere. 'Let me go! How dare you? Let me go!' She was still bleating protests like a record needle stuck in a groove as Hugh marched her along the footpath at a run and propelled her roughly up the steps to his front door.

He gave several quick thumps with the door-knocker and kept the bruising grip on her arm while they stood waiting for someone to let them in. Lindsay had given up struggling; it was undignified—not to say utterly futile.

'Good evening, Mr Rydon,' said the middle-aged woman who opened the door—presumably, Hugh's housekeeper. Unsurprised, she stood aside to let them in, giving Lindsay an incurious glance as Hugh all but hauled her into the hall. 'Will you be wanting supper?' she asked as if it were a regular occurence for her employer to march his dates home for a snack.

'I'll let you know later. Thank you, Mrs Holland,' Hugh replied with a polite, but very definite dismissal in his voice, and, opening the sitting-room door, gave Lindsay a push into the room. He released her once he'd slammed the door shut, but didn't move away from it. 'Right,' he ground out in checked fury. 'Now repeat what you said in the car.'

Lindsay eyed him sullenly. 'I don't remember,' she lied, and had to give a jerky little skip to the side to escape the reach of the arm that shot out at her. 'Don't you dare touch me again, you . . . brute,' she hissed, pointedly rubbing her upper arm where Hugh's fingers had bit into it through the sleeve of her coat.

Hugh dropped his arm with an angry flap. 'I wasn't going to hurt you,' he muttered, following the movement of her hand with a glare. 'I just want you to tell me again what you said in the car.'

'You heard me the first time,' Lindsay mumbled

evasively, and then, as Hugh's scowl blackened, something happened inside her head—a sort of flick of a mental switch and her anger snapped on . . . sharp, cold, and very deadly, with nothing of the helpless frustration about it that had diluted it into white-faced misery during their drive from the hotel. Lindsay felt her mouth twisting into an arch of pure hostility. 'All right then, let's make an issue of it, since that's what you want—and of course, what Hugh Rydon wants goes, doesn't it?' she jeered for openers. 'I said, I did not have an affair with Charles in Sydney, and I'm not having one with him now, whatever that peacock of a cousin of yours is trying to make out. And for your further information, I wouldn't touch that conscienceless rogue with a twenty-foot barge-pole, so does that make me enough of a goody two-shoes for you?' Eyes glittering venom, Lindsay watched the progression of expressions across Hugh's face, from the quick flash of surprise . . . the frown . . . to the comprehension edging slowly into his eyes, and knew that he believed her.

'Then why in heaven's name didn't you have the sense to tell me that before?' Hugh shouted, making Lindsay burst out with an involuntary laugh.

Had she really expected him to be abashed, to fall over himself apologising for all the rotten things he'd assumed about her? How naïve could you get? 'Oh-oh, here we go again: *you* jump to the conclusions, and *I* have to justify them.'

'Damn it, Lindsay, you could have explained ages ago,' Hugh growled, showing sudden colour at her gibe, and just possibly at his own pig-headed unreason.

'Why?' Lindsay spat the word out with venom. 'So that you could be sure I was worthy to be honoured with your attentions? That I was good enough for you?' A quiver ran unevenly through her voice as her anger shot up about a hundred degrees. 'What beats me is how you could have possibly taken me to meet your friends last Sunday. You must have been worried sick I'd show you up by latching on to the first husband I came across, or something.'

Hugh was shaking his head and looking at her as if she was stark raving mad. Perhaps she was, but Lindsay hadn't finished yet. 'And why in blazes did you hire me at all, that's what I'd like to know, when you were so convinced I was carrying on with Charles—a shameless little marriage-breaker, and you so concerned for your sister?' The flare of anger was burning itself out into a confusion of bitterness and hurt.

Hugh was still shaking his head—mechanically, as if he had forgotten he was doing it. 'Haven't you understood anything?' he asked, slowly, incredulous. 'Don't you understand? I'm crazy about you. I've been crazy about you since the first moment you stormed into my office like a fury.'

'That is a lie!' Lindsay shot back in a hiss, her hurt too raw to let him get away with a stretch of the truth for whatever reason, even if her mind had taken in what Hugh had just told her, which it hadn't. 'You thought I was marriage-wrecker, and a blackmailer into the bargain,' she reminded him belligerently, and Hugh flushed, suddenly and deeply.

'Only for the first few moments,' he qualified her angry reminder defensively. 'And then I couldn't really believe it . . . that you had been taken in by Charles' facile, worn-out charm. It just didn't seem possible; until your accident, when I simply didn't know what to think.'

'It was just that—an accident. And it was your fault anyway,' Lindsay accused him heatedly, if irrationally. 'You made me so mad, I didn't stop to look where I was going when I rushed out of the place.'

'I know. Now. But then . . .' Hugh grimaced. 'When the hospital telephoned, I was frantic about you. And later, frantic that you'd up and fly back to Australia. I had to hope the lure of working for Ruytons would keep you here, but I was so damned scared it might have been the lure of Charles. I just couldn't be sure, Lindsay.' Hugh's eyes pleaded for understanding. 'It wasn't you having had affairs —you could have had dozens, I don't care a jot,' he assured her with urgent earnestness. 'It was the not knowing if there was something going on between you and Charles that was driving me insane with jealousy. I couldn't bear the thought of not having a chance with you when I was so crazy about you. *Am* crazy about you,' he amended the tense with a warm smile. 'As crazy about you as you are about me,' Hugh added, his smile curving knowingly, and then changing into an amused laugh as Lindsay rose to the bait and opened her mouth for the reflex, knee-jerk denial.

'I am not . . .' The vehement protest didn't get finished, because Hugh reached out to her suddenly and pulled her to him roughly, wrapped his arms around her and kissed her—hard, without preamble and without tenderness. And Lindsay responded with a passion that matched his, but with an anger that was all her own.

She flung her arms around his shoulders and dug her fingers into the back of his neck, wanting to hurt . . . wanting to pay him back for every bit of hurt he had caused her. Hugh made a satisfied groaning sound into her lips as if the pressure of her angry fingers delighted him, and then, impatiently, brought his hands to the front of her coat, pulling it open and reaching inside to wrap his arms around her again, bringing her hard against himself, leaning into her bruisingly through the soft wool jersey of her dress as if determined she should be aware of his arousal—the urgent need that was setting off an answering need of her own.

With a flare of age-old feminine triumph, Lindsay crushed herself fiercely against him in unsatisfied yearning, aching with a real physical pain for more than the pressure of his body against her . . . much more.

Hugh pulled his mouth away, keeping her locked tightly in his arms, and looking deeply into her eyes as he pressed the flat of his palms under the round curves of her buttocks, watching her through half-closed eyes as Lindsay reacted with a sharp indrawn gasp against the renewed piercing ache that shot through her.

'Now, what was it you wanted to say . . . ? Something about not being crazy about me, wasn't it?' Hugh teased softly, while all the time his hands kept their deliberate sensuous pressure under her coat.

Lindsay let out a tiny, breathless laugh, and made a protesting movement of her head. Not crazy about him? Every throb, every ache was a confirmation of the craziness that made her feel a stranger to herself . . . vulnerable to Hugh's every touch . . . passionate—more totally a woman than she had ever felt. And somewhere, a long way back in her mind, afraid. It was as if she really had gone a little crazy—more than a little, but well and truly crazy, wanting to give herself to a man she had barely known three weeks, and without a thought to those old-fashioned ideals Charles had laughed at—love . . . commitment. Hugh Rydon wasn't offering her anything.

'Well? What now, darling?' Hugh asked cryptically, watching her face carefully.

What now, indeed? Lindsay looked back at him without an answer.

'Shall I ask Mrs Holland to rustle up some supper for us, or would you prefer to make it to the theatre for the second half of the show?'

Two ordinary, matter-of-fact choices. On the surface. Lindsay looked beneath the surface and saw the fire in the grate, Hugh's long, lean frame stretched out on the rug; saw herself alongside him, his arms around her as they were in this long, intimate embrace . . . And then beyond. She trembled suddenly and violently against him. 'Supper,' she said very softly, closing her mind off to the enormity of her decision, and her eyes against the fierce glow that sprang into Hugh's eyes as he bent his face to her for a kiss.

'I promise you I won't be falling asleep this time,' he murmured into her lips, and drew back sharply as the brisk tap broke the soft warm silence. 'Yes?' Hugh called out tersely, keeping his arms around her.

Mrs Holland opened the door and stood in the doorway, the same incurious expression on her face—her standard expression, thought Lindsay, blushing and pulling herself hurriedly out of Hugh's arms.

'There you are, Mrs Holland,' Hugh smiled, completely unembarrassed. 'I was just about to go looking for you,' he lied blandly. 'I think we're ready for some supper now, if you wouldn't mind.'

The housekeeper's expression did change then; very subtly . . . a mere tensing of the muscles. 'Certainly, Mr Rydon,' she answered, then remained standing just inside the door.

'Yes, Mrs Holland? Is there something else?' Hugh asked, a note of impatience in his voice.

'I think you might wish to know that there has been a telephone call for you,' Mrs Holland said, solemnly, and with an air of passing on a secret message.

Hugh frowned, perplexed. 'You said I wasn't available?'

'I did, but . . .' the housekeeper hesitated.

'But . . . ?' Hugh prompted with sharpness, and

even Lindsay was curious at the housekeeper's odd reticence.

Mrs Holland glanced briefly at Lindsay and back to her employer. 'But,' she repeated with emphasis, 'Mrs Rydon felt you might wish to see her none the less.'

There was a long silence, perhaps meaningful, only not to Lindsay. She felt a sudden surprise that Charles' wife should be contacting Hugh before recollecting that she was his sister, but even then it did seem a little strange at this time of night.

'I see,' Hugh said tonelessly, but Lindsay didn't miss the seizing up of the jawline, nor the flash of what looked like anger across his face. 'Will you excuse me for a moment?' He gave her a brief, distracted smile and left the room with Mrs Holland, leaving Lindsay wondering what was going on.

Did the housekeeper mean the woman wanted to come to see Hugh now? Had something happened to Charles? Lindsay couldn't begin to think of an explanation, and it wasn't her business, anyway.

Hugh returned so quickly, she suspected he had had whatever discussion with his housekeeper just outside the door. There was a change in him, a jerky nervousness about him, and Lindsay knew what he was going to say before he said it.

'Darling, I'm sorry. Something has cropped up rather unexpectedly.' Hugh smiled ruefully, coming to her. 'I'm afraid we're going to have to take a rain-check on our supper.'

'That's all right,' Lindsay assured him, over-brightly, while her heart plummeted in disappointment. 'It doesn't matter.' She turned from him quickly and went to the armchair to get her bag.

Hugh came up behind her. 'Of course it matters,' he contradicted her vehemently, and, taking her by the shoulders, drew her to himself hungrily. 'I want you. I want to make love to you. You want that too, don't you?' he demanded huskily, his eyes burning her with their fire. 'Don't you?' Hugh repeated urgently when Lindsay didn't answer straight away. 'For heaven's sake, answer me, Lindsay. I haven't got it all wrong, have I? You did want to stay here tonight and make love, didn't you?' Hugh's voice went suddenly uncertain on the last question, matching the uncertainty that flooded into his eyes as they searched her face for an answer.

Her nod was the tiniest movement of the head. 'Yes,' Lindsay admitted at last in a small whisper, and saw the doubt clear from Hugh's eyes, felt the tremor of relief run through his body as he held her closely. Their final kiss was achingly sweet and fierce at the same time, and all too short. Hugh broke it off abruptly.

'We'll have all the time in the world, darling, when I get back from New York. I did mention that I'm going, didn't I?' he asked sharply as Lindsay's eyes clouded. 'Tomorrow afternoon. I must, darling—it's to do with the branch of Ruytons we're setting up over there. It'll be a fortnight at the most—less, if I can manage it. And think of the prospective new market for your designs, 'he added, smiling, trying to tease her out of the disappointment that must have been written all over her face.

Lindsay pulled herself together with an effort and forced out a hurried smile. 'That'll be wonderful,' she said, very brightly, and eased herself away from him. 'You'd better call me a cab now, don't you think?' she suggested briskly.

'I've already asked Mrs Holland to do that. It should be here any moment. I'm sorry, Lindsay. It's just that . . .' Hugh broke off with an uncomfortable shrug, and later in the taxi Lindsay wondered if she had imagined the evasiveness about him, the edginess as they had waited for the taxi to arrive.

Understandable, if his sister was about to turn up on the doorstep in a state, Lindsay pointed out to herself. And something had to be amiss for her to be needing to see Hugh so late on a Saturday night, and it would have been awkward and embarrassing for everybody if she had arrived to find a stranger with her brother.

As the piercing disappointment at the way the evening had ended started to fade, Lindsay wasn't sure whether she was glad or sorry that fate had intervened so unexpectedly. At least now she had time to try to put her feelings into some sort of perspective—disturbing feelings, irrational, and not something Lindsay was used to in herself.

Hugh had said he was crazy about her, and somehow, while wrapped in his arms, his being 'crazy' about her had seemed enough. But was it? What had Hugh really meant? Nothing more than crazy to get her into bed. And she had been just as crazy to land up in there with him.

Sex or love . . . ? Did it matter? Lindsay watched

the frenetic activity of a busy London Saturday
night from the window of the cab as it wove its way
through the heavy traffic towards Bayswater. No,
it didn't matter—not for the moment. Later,
perhaps, she would find herself wanting the
commitment . . . the fidelity—the love she had
always believed a relationship should be based on.
And later, perhaps, Hugh might offer her all those
things. Or was she being naïve . . . romantic?
Lindsay couldn't tell. All she knew was that she
couldn't get Hugh out of her mind; he was part of
her every waking moment during the next week and
she couldn't believe she could miss anybody so
much, let alone someone she had known such a
short time.

'I knew it, Lindsay, you are in love,' Kelly
pronounced with relish during one of their evening
meals together. But then, Kelly had a one-track
mind.

Was she in love, though? Lindsay wondered. She
had never been in love, and couldn't associate the
crazy yo-yoing feelings with love now. Up sky-high
one moment, down in the pits of gloom the next. It
didn't make sense and couldn't be love, yet every
other evening, when Hugh telephoned her at the
hotel, she went flying down the stairs on wings, not
feet, uncaring of Mrs Layton hanging about the
foyer, ears flapping. And then, each time, Lindsay
went back upstairs, flushed and happy, Hugh's
voice still tingling in her ear telling her he was
missing her.

And in between Hugh's calls the days dragged

leadenly, her spark gone, and it was certain Edwards must have noticed her lack of progress on the re-design of the piece they had selected as the first of her collection, only Edwards, being Edwards, made no comment.

Ruytons itself was buzzing with pre-exhibition fever at the start of the second week of Hugh's absence. 'The place goes haywire,' Hugh had told her, and hadn't been far off the mark with his description. Everybody was running about, pieces were being cleaned, last-minute alterations made, and Charles was all over the place—in his element ordering everyone about. But avoiding her, very pointedly, Lindsay noticed, wryly amused and suspecting that Hugh might have been responsible for his cousin's new, distant manner. The trouble was, she found Charles' careful offhandedness —high-handedness—almost as irritating as his overbearing intimacy had been.

'Do make sure Kelly turns up on time this evening,' he told her officiously as Lindsay was getting ready to go home on the day of the exhibition.

Lindsay snapped her teeth together and gave them a little grind to give herself a moment before answering coolly, 'I'm sure Kelly will manage to get herself there on time.'

'Yes, well . . .' Charles muttered. 'Well, I'll see you there,' he smiled on an afterthought.

Not if I see you first, Lindsay retorted in her head. 'Yes, probably. Goodnight, Charles,' she said quite pleasantly, and walked out of the workshop before she gave in to temptation and snapped his head off.

It was not her responsibility to see that Kelly got anywhere on time; she had done her bit by introducing them, after a fashion, and didn't have any further interest in their arrangements, although she knew Kelly had met Charles again and had been to a rehearsal last week, because Kelly had come home in raptures over the jewels, and over-awed by the security arrangements that went with them. Not surprising, considering the combined value of the gems to be shown, and that was without counting the jewels strung around the necks of the female half of the guests who were paying a fortune to come and look at more. All in a good cause, of course.

'Oxfam or something.' Charles had been vague about that part of it, but that hadn't stopped him conveying the impression that whoever the recipient was, they would have him to thank for the boost to their funds. Vanity again, Lindsay surmised acidly, still annoyed at his officiousness, which must have been due, in part at least, to nerves, because, love the excitement of it all as he did, Charles was as wound up as a clockwork toy. She supposed it was natural he would worry about models turning up on time, especially since he didn't really know Kelly and wouldn't realise the dear girl would probably turn up hours before anyone else.

Only Lindsay was wrong. Kelly opened her door and crept out on to the landing as Lindsay climbed up the last flight of stairs.

'Lindsay . . .' she croaked, looking as if she was about to cry. She was in her dressing-gown and had a thick scarf wound around her neck.

Lindsay stared, horrified.

'Look . . .' Kelly ordered huskily, unpeeling the scarf. 'I woke up this morning and there they were.'

Lindsay looked in disbelief at the two enormous lumps that distorted the fine shape of Kelly's long neck. 'Oh, no . . . your glands. Oh, Kelly!' she wailed, not knowing whether to laugh or cry at this awful twist of bad luck. One look at Kelly's miserable face scotched the idea of trying to laugh it off as a joke. 'Are you all right?' Lindsay asked in concern. 'Have you called in a doctor?'

Kelly shook her head glumly. 'I thought they would go away,' she whispered, fingering her throat gingerly. 'I stayed in bed all day and kept warm, and took dozens of aspirins. Do you think anyone will notice?' she appealed pathetically, tears in her eyes.

'Yes, Kelly, I'm afraid they will.' Lindsay smiled a little in spite of herself at the picture of Charles having a fit if Kelly turned up—on time, granted, but with a throat almost twice its normal size. 'You know you can't model necklaces with a throat like that, darling,' she pointed out gently. 'And you shouldn't be out of bed,' Lindsay added, suspecting that the glistening brightness in Kelly's eyes was due to fever as much as tears of misery. 'Put your scarf back on and go back to bed, and I'll telephone Charles for you. He should still be at Ruytons.'

Charles himself answered on the nightline extension in the workshop, and swore with furious abandon when Lindsay told him, very matter-of-factly, that Kelly was ill.

'Then why in blazes didn't the wretched girl let me know earlier?' he demanded with petulant anger.

'Because "the wretched girl" was dosing herself almost into a coma hoping to get the infection down so she wouldn't let you down, that's why,' Lindsay barked into her ear. 'You'll just have to get the other girls to do Kelly's pieces.'

'I can't,' Charles told her in a high-pitched wail. 'They've got their work cut out as it is. We need a third girl. You'll have to do it, Lindsay.'

'No way, Charles. I can't . . .' Lindsay went on to protest and set her own trap.

'Lindsay, darling, for Ruytons,' Charles appealed, cunningly, she realised later. 'And of course you can do it—you've done it before, when you modelled your own pendant at that Sydney do. You were fabulous.' Charles paused for her response. Lindsay stayed silent. 'Lindsay, be reasonable. It's simply not possible to get anyone else at an hour's notice. You must help us out.'

'Us . . . Ruytons'. Not a 'me' in the whole sentence.

'Well . . .' Lindsay wavered.

'Black dress. Long and slinky, and as little of it up top as decency allows,' Charles instructed crisply. 'Like the one you wore in Sydney. Bring it with you?' he fired at her.

'Yes,' Lindsay replied without thinking.

'Great. Be there at seven. Tell the security men to come and get me, otherwise they won't let you in to the back room. It's like Fort Knox in there. Oh, and Lindsay, hair up, please. I want it sleek . . . very ophisticated.' The phone was dropped down in her ear.

Half amused, half angry at Charles' instant solution, Lindsay went back upstairs and told Kelly what was happening. 'Sorry, Kelly. I know how much you were looking forward to it all.' Lindsay felt awful—as if she had somehow cheated her friend out of a plum job, which was nonsense and they both knew it.

'More blusher when you get there, otherwise the lights will make you look washed out,' Kelly advised when Lindsay came in to say goodnight. 'You do look gorgeous,' Kelly added with good-natured sincerity, then eyed Lindsay's ubiquitous navy wool coat with a dubious frown. 'But you do need a fur coat, darling.'

'Chance would be a fine thing—and I don't approve of them anyway,' Lindsay retorted with a smile. 'Stay warm and try and get some sleep. I won't wake you when I come in, but I'll drop in first thing tomorrow morning and tell you all about it,' she promised.

CHAPTER NINE

THE large, ornate clock in the foyer of the gran
hotel which was the venue of the exhibition showe
ten minutes to seven, but Charles was already pacin
agitatedly beside the two security men who had set u
a sort of checkpoint at the front end of a wide, lon
corridor which gave off the foyer.

'Here you are at last,' he called out impatiently a
Lindsay approached, and sounded as if she had kep
him waiting for hours. 'It's all right, chaps, Lindsa
is one of my girls,' he told the security men, blithel
patronising and setting Lindsay's teeth on edge
'Replacement for Kelly Jordan. Lindsay Warren i
the name. Tick her off, I can vouch for her.'

'Lucky you.' The younger of the guards grinne
appreciatively and recorded something against the lis
of names on his desk.

Charles bustled her along the corridor at breath
taking speed. 'You look super, darling.' He flicke
an appraising eye over her hair, sleekly piled to th
back of her head. 'Exactly as I wanted. Here we are.
He brought them to an abrupt halt half-way dow
the corridor. 'Number five, that's us, the Ruyton
room; we've all got one each,' he explained, giving
sharp tap on the door which was opened by ye
another security guard, and there were still anothe

154

couple inside with the two stunning-looking girls who were Ruytons models for the evening. Kelly had been right when she said the place was crawling with security men; and there would be dozens more mingling among the guests in the ballroom.

Charles waved a breezy hand towards the two girls. 'Introductions later, girls. Take your coat off now, Lindsay,' he ordered. 'You'll warm up in a minute. I need to look at you.'

Lindsay took the coat off and Charles looked, and it wasn't at all a quick, professional once-over. it was lingering and intense, and Lindsay felt herself going red with embarrassment and annoyance at the blatantly sexual appraisal.

'No wonder cousin Hugh has ordered me off the territory,' Charles murmured with a suggestive smile.

'Oh, put a sock in it, Charles,' Lindsay snapped at him and glanced around the room. There was another door which presumably gave access to the ballroom, but that wasn't what she wanted. She moved back to the door they had just come in through. 'I need to go out again for a moment, please,' she told the guard at the door.

'Now? Why?' Charles yelped behind her.

'For heaven's sake, I only want to go to the loo. I'm not about to try running off with the collection,' Lindsay muttered at him. 'And I can manage alone, thank you.' She froze him off with a glare, not putting it past Charles to trail out with her.

She was coming along the corridor on her way

back when she saw Hugh coming around the
guards' desk and walking towards her, unhurried-
ly, a tall, dark figure, so devastatingly handsome in
his dark formal suit that Lindsay went weak at the
knees. She just stood there and stared for a long
moment before breaking into a run and flying to
meet him.

She stopped suddenly a few paces from him to
stop herself from hurling herself into his arms.
'Hugh,' she laughed, tinklingly, as confused as a
schoolgirl unexpectedly faced with her crush.

Hugh's eyes drifted over her, slowly, top to
bottom, as if he had never seen her before. He
hadn't, either, Lindsay realised. Not like this.
Every time they'd been together to date, she had
been dressed ever so sensibly; even the sexy black
cashmere had covered her from neck to knee,
unlike this slinky silk . . . slashed in a straight line
low across her breasts, with a tiny strap over each
shoulder its sole support. A daft thing to wear on a
freezing night.

Hugh's admiration was as blatant as Charles'
had been, and every bit as sexual, but Lindsay
thought it wonderful. She was tingling all over
when their eyes met again.

'You're beautiful,' Hugh said thickly, his eyes
devouring her.

Lindsay flushed searingly with pleasure, and
wanted to tell him he looked beautiful, too.
'Thank you,' she murmured shyly, then laughed
delightedly. 'What are you doing here? Back from
New York so soon? I thought you said you

wouldn't be back until the weekend. It's only Wednesday.'

'I couldn't wait to get back to you,' Hugh replied softly, predictably. 'I missed you so much.' Lines from a rotten movie, and Lindsay had never heard anything more romantic. 'I called in at your plce on my way in from Heathrow and spoke to Mrs Layton, who told me the latest turn of events—with gusto,' Hugh added with a chuckle. 'Then I looked in on poor old Kelly, raced home and changed, and here I am.'

'How stoic of you. I distinctly remember you telling me that you never came to this sort of thing,' Lindsay teased gently.

'Wild horses would not have kept me away tonight,' Hugh said, predictably again. 'Will you have supper with me this evening—after your bit is over?'

'I'm last on the billing. Ruytons is the last of the exhibitors and Kelly was to model the last pieces,' Lindsay explained hurriedly and breathlessly, shy of saying "yes" to the supper that was just a euphemism for what Hugh had in mind.

'I'll wait.' Hugh lifted her chin up with a forefinger and brought his mouth to her lips, and Lindsay felt an instantaneous warm explosion of desire at the contact.

She brushed his hand away and wrapped her arms wildly around his neck, kissing him hungrily, a week and a half of longing pouring out of her. Hugh's arms circled her waist, crushing her to him.

'Was that a "yes"?' he asked with a mock frown

when they finally broke apart. His hands stayed around her, lightly stroking the curve of he hips.

How could he ask, teasingly or otherwise? There was no way she could have said 'no' to him. It was insane to feel this way about any man: that nothing mattered but to be with him. Hugh's brief absence had proved that to her as nothing else could have; proved to her, too, that she was madly, wonderfully in love with him. 'Yes, oh yes,' Lindsay gave a breathless, happy laugh.

'For Pete's sake, Lindsay,' Charles yelled querulously from somewhere behind her. 'Hugh, get your hands off her this instant. You'll mess up her dress.'

'The master's voice,' Hugh grinned. 'You'd better not keep him waiting. Charles does tend to get a bit snappy when he's in a flap.'

'I've noticed,' Lindsay grinned back, extricating herself reluctantly from the warm circle of Hugh's arms and giving her dress a quick smooth-down.

Hugh watched, the look in his eyes telling her that he had the dress off her already. Lindsay went pink.

'You can read my mind beautifully,' Hugh laughed softly. 'That's exactly what I want to do.'

'Lindsay!'

'I'm coming, Charles.' Lindsay flashed Hugh a last radiant smile and hurried down the corridor to the irate Charles, conscious of Hugh's eyes following her every curve through the thin silk of the dress.

'Talk about no sense of timing,' Charles muttered peevishly. 'What is he doing back so soon, anyway?' he asked belligerently.

'He missed me,' Lindsay returned sweetly, utterly immune to Charles' sour temper and everything else about him. Hugh was back; she was madly, rapturously in love, and nothing could penetrate the warm, insulating glow that made her feel she was floating on air when her turn came to be decked out in Ruytons' most fabulous pieces and waft into the ballroom, a spotlight trained on her to highlight the armoury of jewels she was showing off.

Lindsay drifted . . . paused . . . smiled—did everything Charles had instructed, then returned to the changing-room to have a different set of gems hung around her before wafting out again to drift . . . pause . . . smile.

She was aware of sharp intakes of breath . . . little hisses of disbelief and envy . . . of oohs and aahs—all par for the course. It was a rare woman who could restrain the involuntary gasps when faced with the proverbial king's ransom in gems, and an even rarer one who didn't crave a share of them.

And then, at last, Charles was settling the opal pendant around her neck which meant her last foray into the audience.

'Did I tell you Natalie wanted this?' he murmured as he fiddled—too long, at her bosom. 'She tried to make me give her this one when she saw it, but Hugh wouldn't hear of it. So now she wants you to make another just like it.' Charles stood back and gave her a quick look up and down.

Lindsay smiled at him tightly. 'Tell your wife I only design one-offs.'

Charles shot up one eyebrow, a faintly malicious

smile playing about his lips. 'My wife? No, darling—Hugh's. Don't tell me he hasn't mentioned the lovely Natalie to you? No?' The smile intensified as Lindsay's face showed her shock. 'Then you must ask him about her some time. Off you go, now.' He gave her a little shove towards the door. 'And do put your smile back on, Lindsay, it's slipped off.'

The room was a blur when she went out again. She supposed she must have smiled in the best tradition of 'the show must go on'; certainly her mouth was aching when she wafted her way back to the exit for the last time to the accompaniment of a round of applause, and found Hugh waiting there for her, smiling the warm, intimate smile that had made her go weak at the knees—still made her go weak at the knees.

To her own amazement, Lindsay felt her mouth curving into a reciprocal smile.

'You were wonderful,' Hugh told her softly, bending his head to her ear in what could only have been construed as a loving gesture by anyone who happened to observe it.

'Thank you, darling,' Lindsay fairly cooed, widening the smile and putting a hand on Hugh's arm—possessively . . . intimately. 'Are you ready to leave now?' She looked him steadily in the eyes. 'For our supper?' she reminded him with a suggestive giggle, and noted the flash of perplexed surprise in Hugh's eyes at her bluntness.

'Is everything all right, Lindsay?' he asked, with a faint frown, looking her over carefully.

'Super,' she trilled. 'I'll just go and get my coat,

shall I?' She took her hand off his arm. 'Oh, and I'd better give them back this pendant, or the security brigade will be sending a posse after us.' Lindsay laughed excessively at her own fatuous humour.

Hugh didn't even smile. 'It doesn't need to go back. It's yours. You made it, I bought it—not Ruytons. For you. I meant to tell you that before,' he told her, still without a smile but with that watchful look in his eyes.

Lindsay recharged the brilliance of her own smile. 'Why, thank you, darling,' she breathed huskily in a parody of being thrilled. 'Only I haven't done anything to earn it—yet—have I?' She stared up at him, all wide-eyed ingénue, and saw Hugh's colour darken in the sudden flush that swept over his stony face. 'I'll get my coat.' Lindsay left him hurriedly, as much flabbergasted by her own behaviour as Hugh was, and scared out of her wits because she had as little control over what was coming out of her mouth as a ventriloquist's dummy. The awful words, laughter, simply kept popping out, unconnected to anything inside her head, possibly because her mind had gone into self-protective shock at Charles' cunningly timed announcement, temporarily repressing the mountain of anger and misery that would eventually have to explode out of her when it really hit home that she had fallen for what she had always considered the worst type of creep—the married man playing around behind his wife's back.

And Hugh was just that: just another married man . . . another Charles, and like countless others of his ilk. Yet she was going to go to bed with him. The

certainty horrified her, scared her out of her mind.
Just this once, Lindsay begged herself, pleading
against cold reason as she walked down the corridor
towards Hugh, and felt she was going to her own
execution.

Hugh waited for her, unsmiling, and Lindsay
didn't smile either as she reached him, looking at him
as if he was a stranger—which, in fact, was what he
was: a stranger with a life she didn't know anything
about . . . could never be part of. So much for her
hopes—fantasies—that their relationship was leading
somewhere. Oh, it was leading somewhere all
right—to bed tonight, and misery and self-disgust
tomorrow.

Who cares? Lindsay dismissed tomorrow grimly.
Tonight she wanted Hugh as much as he wanted her,
and if she couldn't have his love then she would settle
for whatever he was offering.

'I'm ready,' she announced with a ghost of a
smile.

'Are you sure?' Hugh's eyes reached into hers
searchingly.

Lindsay flicked her eyes away. 'Oh, yes, I'm sure,'
she assured him with a jangling little laugh, and
slipped her hand through his arm.

In the car, she didn't look at him once; she stared
straight ahead, humming tunelessly under her breath,
her mind quite blank. 'Goodness, are we here
already?' Lindsay feigned bright astonishment when
Hugh pulled up outside his house.

He slipped the key out of the ignition, but didn't
make any move to open the door. 'What's wrong,

Lindsay?' he appealed with a low urgency.

Every damned thing, you double-crossing, lying rat, Lindsay wanted to scream at him. She gave an airy toss of her head. 'Not a thing. Shall we go in?' She opened her door without waiting for him and hopped out, and was running lightly up his steps when Hugh caught up with her. 'Your wife isn't planning to drop in this evening, is she?' Lindsay asked, offhandedly, and heard Hugh draw in his breath with a hiss.

'What is that supposed to mean?' he asked, very tightly.

Lindsay turned an innocent smile to him. 'Well, I mean . . .' she gave a silly little giggle. 'It might be a bit awkward for us . . . like the other night—when you had to scuttle me off before she got here. It was Natalie about to descend, wasn't it?' It hadn't been Charles' wife, but Hugh's own, Lindsay was sure of that now. No wonder Hugh couldn't get her out of the place quickly enough. There had been other signs as well, only she had been too thick to take them in . . . Philip's mention of a Mrs Hugh Rydon, which she had not taken literally . . . Charles' earlier remark about Natalie wanting to see Hugh.

Hugh muttered something angrily under his breath as he unlocked the door, and Lindsay stepped in, almost gaily, into the lighted hall.

'Look, Lindsay, I'm sorry about the other night,' Hugh said tersely. 'Is that why you've suddenly gone all . . . uptight?' he asked sharply, and might have said 'peculiar' which was what Lindsay knew he meant. 'It won't happen again, Lindsay,' Hugh insisted with angry earnestness. 'I promise you. The other night was just one of those things,' he added with a shrug.

A wife popping by and interrupting an illicit evening with a girlfriend was 'just one of those things'? What sort of man was Hugh? Lindsay doubted even Charles could have been so insensitively crass about it. Or was Hugh being just too sophisticated for her? She stared at him, quite impressed in a shocked sort of way at how some men 'operated', but sick inside that she wanted this particular 'operator' . . . was so crazy about him that she was prepared to trade in her self-respect and all her principles for one night of lovemaking. Go now, a hundred voices yelled in her head, and Lindsay half turned towards the door.

'Lindsay—darling . . .' Hugh suddenly reached out to her and took her into his arms, and the voices stopped dead without a whimper. Just this once, her body urged her on as Lindsay lifted her face for Hugh's kiss.

'Not here,' Hugh murmured thickly, and with an arm tightly around her shoulder he led her through the hall and up the curved staircase. 'Mrs Holland is away. She wasn't expecting me back for another couple of days.'

And neither was Natalie, it seemed, who must also have taken herself off somewhere during Hugh's absence—probably their standard arrangement. 'How lovely to have the house to ourselves,' Lindsay heard herself trill coyly, and hated herself, but knew she was going to hate herself a whole lot more.

The lamp on the small round table in the corner of the bedroom was on, its reddish shade casting a warm, diffused colour into the room that was plain to the point of being spare. Lindsay noted this with faint surprise, and then wondered whether Natalie Rydon had her own separate, and no doubt ultra-feminine, room next door. That was the way sophisticated people lived, wasn't it? Separate rooms . . . separate lives. And Hugh was as sophisticated as they came—treating an extra-marital affair as a commonplace occurrence in his life, and expecting her to feel the same way about something which to Lindsay was the most shattering experience she was ever likely to have. Naïve . . . unsophisticated goody two-shoes. She understood now why Hugh had reassured her so vehemently that he didn't care if she'd had dozens of previous lovers.

Lindsay smiled bitterly to herself, then hurriedly changed the curve of the smile as Hugh lifted his hand from her shoulder to the side of her head and turned her face towards him.

'Let me take my coat off,' Lindsay murmured with a scratchy laugh, and then felt she was performing a strip-tease as she removed her coat watched by those dark and glittery eyes—with an anger about them too, she thought, nervously, tossing the coat over the nearest chair.

'I'm not sure I understand you, Lindsay,' Hugh watched her every move with an intensity Lindsay found scary.

'Then perhaps you shouldn't try,' she quipped with a pathetic attempt to tease, and moved

seductively towards him, her hands raised to twine
around his neck, and undulating her hips
provocatively. She felt for a moment like a trained
whore, and was appalled at herself.

Hugh caught up her hands by the wrists and
brought them down firmly to her sides and left them
there, his eyes holding her immobile while he untied
his bow-tie with a deft flick of the wrist, pulled it out
from under his collar and tossed it aside without
looking to see where it dropped, going on to
unbutton his shirt with slow, deliberate fingers, and
watching her face as she watched his hands. When
Lindsay raised her eyes he smiled at her faintly, a
measured sensuousness in the curve of his lips, and
something inside her went cold.

This was not the way she had thought it was going
to be; not the way she could bring herself to commit
adultery . . . or was Hugh, being married, the
adulterer . . . ? Crushed in his arms, senses aflame
and mind . . . mindless, yes, but not like this . . . not
with this pointedly deliberate preparation, each
other's every move almost pruriently observed.

'What's the matter, Lindsay?' Hugh asked softly,
leaving the shirt only half unbuttoned and placing his
hands lightly on her shoulders—to hold her away
from contact with his body while he took her mouth
in a controlled, insistent kiss with no passion in it.

Lindsay responded, her mind unwilling, but her
lips parting instantly on the flare of involuntary
arousal which made her try to reach against him,
only to be restrained by the hands on her shoulders
keeping her firmly, tantalisingly back.

With frustrated urgency her mouth pleaded for passion, and then, when Hugh broke off the unsatisfying kiss completely, Lindsay gave a little whimper of protest, turning it in the next breath into a gratified sigh as Hugh began to kiss her slowly down her throat. She arched her throat back, reaching her hands into his hair and trembling as his mouth found the throbbing pulse in the curve of her neck just above the swirl of pendant. It lingered there tormentingly before setting off again along the line of one shoulder and leaving a warm, moist trail where it touched.

'Hugh . . . please . . .' Lindsay drew his head up agitatedly, and Hugh's lips were smiling as they descended on her waiting mouth, but still without the passion she wanted—needed from him to keep her doubts at bay.

She felt his hands slip around her, unerringly locate the tag of the invisible zipper in the back of her dress and draw it down slowly, the sound of it cutting through the room and into Lindsay's consciousness.

She made an agitated movement of her head—a protest from her rational mind at what he was doing—but Hugh chose that moment to harden the pressure of his mouth, his probing tongue expertly eliciting the mindless surge of passion from her, and the feeble protest died unheeded.

The tiny straps slid over her shoulders, and then Lindsay felt Hugh's fingers touching warm, bare skin as they peeled the black silk over the roundness of her breasts and eased it down to her waist. She was naked underneath. Lindsay's eyes snapped open and saw

Hugh's already open and watching eyes, and she gasped into his mouth with sheer pleasure as each breast was taken into a rounded palm and just held.

Hugh pulled his mouth away and kept watching her through heavy, half-closed lids as he moved his hands slightly to position his thumbs at the hardened projecting nipples and began to tease them rhythmically, leaning his body into her at last, a small smile lifting the corner of his mouth as he watched her eyes stretch wide into shock.

The wave of violent, trembling sensation started somewhere deep and low inside her and rushed through her. And didn't stop. Lindsay clung to Hugh's shoulders, rocked by wave after fiery wave of agonised pleasure that sent her arching and undulating against him in a primitive, mindless rhythm, her head swaying languidly from side to side and her eyelids too heavy to keep open. They shot open again when Hugh bent his head and took one diamond-hard nipple into his mouth.

Lindsay cried out, she didn't know what, and held his head to her, burying her face into the thick, curling hair but unable to stop the cries that seemed to urge Hugh's mouth into more exquisite torture.

And then, suddenly, Hugh raised his head and her hands fell away. He was breathing hard, while Lindsay's shuddering breaths seemed to be drawn from the very depths of her stomach as she watched him looking at her breasts, swollen with arousal and aching for his touch. Very slowly Hugh brought his gaze up to her face, and there was no smile about him any more.

'This is your first time, isn't it,' he stated, not asked, although the form was of a question, and Lindsay's face, already flushed, burned. Her mouth parched, and speech beyond her, she just stared. 'Darling . . . oh, darling.' Hugh engulfed her in his arms suddenly, crushing her to him with all the passion that had been missing from him. He kissed mouth, eyes, and couldn't stop smothering her face with kisses. In the end, he stopped and looked at her again with a tenderness she had never seen before. 'So that's it, darling . . . that's why you were acting so oddly.' Hugh smiled understandingly. 'Trust me, Lindsay. Please trust me, darling. I'll make it wonderful for you.'

There was a new, driven urgency in him now as he shrugged himself out of his jacket and hurled it over a chair, reaching for the buttons he hadn't yet undone on his formal white dress-shirt with eager, impatient fingers, not a trace of the earlier deliberation in them. Throbbing with her own excitement, Lindsay watched breathlessly, and then as Hugh smiled at her lingeringly she swung her face away, a little afraid of the promise blazing in his eyes, and, turning, caught sight of her own reflection in the cheval mirror by the chest of drawers.

Her face . . . body . . . went from burning heat to ice-white cold as she stared at herself . . . eyes enormous and dark with an unnatural glow . . . her lips provocatively full from the assault of Hugh's mouth. Fascinated, horrified, Lindsay slid her gaze down to the heavy swirl of silver curving her neck and sweeping its way down, its black opal nestling

erotically in the shadowy valley between the
voluptuous breasts, their nipples showing darkly
against the creamy smoothness of their background

She was looking at a vision of wantonness . . . a
ripe lusciousness about her. An erotic stranger
Lindsay could barely look at herself, and yet couldn'
draw her appalled eyes away from the sight.

'Now you know why I adore you.'

Hugh's thick, throbbing voice made her tear her
eyes away from the wanton woman in the mirror to
the man who had turned her into one. Hugh was
stripped to his briefs, and Lindsay had never known
that anything could be so threatening and so desirable as the lean, hard-muscled body in front of her.
Her breath quickening again, she ranged her eyes
over Hugh's broad shoulders, wanting desperately to
run her fingers over the smooth brown skin, to
entwine them into the dark, curling hair of his chest.
Her eyes followed its tapering path downwards into
the flat of his stomach and came back up hurriedly as
the wave of sheer physical need rushed through her.
Lindsay closed her eyes for a split second, catching
her breath, and then she flicked them open, shaking
her head wildly.

'No, Hugh,' she whispered, suddenly yanking her
dress up over the exposed breasts before Hugh came
to touch them again. She would be lost then and
utterly in his power, compelled by her own need of
him to surrender her most precious gift to another
woman's husband.

Another woman's husband. All the desire—or was
it lust?—drained out of her, and Lindsay felt weak

with shame. 'I must go home,' she told him agitatedly as she crammed her arms into the little straps and hoisted them over each shoulder while Hugh kept staring at her as if she had gone mad.

Not mad; she had become sane again, she wanted to tell him. The madness had left her, but she couldn't trust it not to return, which was why she was acting as if was a matter of life and death to get herself out of this room—away from this man, while she still could.

'Don't touch me, please,' Lindsay cried out as Hugh moved towards her.

'Lindsay . . .' The one word carried all Hugh's surprise . . . incomprehension . . . bewilderment. Anger.

Lindsay ducked past him, snatched her coat off the chair and thrust herself into it frantically, leaving the back of her dress gaping because it took ages to do up herself and she couldn't have Hugh do it up for her—even had he been willing, which she couldn't risk finding out.

'I'm sorry, Hugh.' Her eyes pleaded into the suddenly stony face; only Hugh's eyes remained expressive—of his anger, and for a moment Lindsay felt really afraid, thought for just that one moment that he would force her to make good her body's erotic promises.

And then Hugh just shook his head as if she was completely beyond his understanding. 'I can't take you home, Lindsay,' he told her in a harsh, grating voice. 'I would end up raping you in the middle of Oxford Street—which . . .' Hugh cut himself off

with an angry shrug, and Lindsay knew the end of
the sentence would have been 'which would be no
more than you deserve.'

CHAPTER TEN

LINDSAY got herself home. She telephoned for a taxi
from Hugh's hall and waited there until it came,
afraid not to, because Hugh had threatened to drive
her home himself, after all, if she made any attempt
to leave the house before the taxi turned up. Lindsay
promised whatever she had to to get out of the room,
leaving Hugh dressing—quickly enough to catch up
with her at the sound of a slamming door if she went
back on her word and ran out of the house into the
night.

Only when she was down in the hall did Lindsay
remember she still had the pendant on—her own
beautiful pendant that she had been so proud of.
Hugh's pendant now; he had bought it, he could
keep it—for a more deserving mistress. Lindsay tore
it off her neck and left it lying on his hall table.

And then, in the taxi, she cried. The tears just kept
streaming down her cheeks in a silent torrent, and
after the first few futile brushes of the hand, Lindsay
let them flow unchecked, not caring if the driver saw
her in his rear-view mirror; not caring about anything
any more. Delayed shock, possibly . . . at finding out
the truth about Hugh . . . at her own near abandon-
ment of her principles for the rapturous, dangerous
pleasure of being made love to by Hugh.

Not love. Expert manipulation of her body. Sex. Love hadn't come into it and never had, and she could have realised that much earlier if she hadn't been so besotted by him. In love. But not loving him, Lindsay tried to persuade herself, and wondered why she bothered, because it could make no difference now how she had felt—still felt about a man she would never see again. And Hugh would never come seeking her out again, either, Lindsay was certain of that. If tonight had proved anything, it was that she simply wasn't mistress material. A hysterical, uptight little virgin waiting for her knight in shining armour, Hugh would think her—if he thought of her again at all.

She arrived back at the hotel after one and must have looked like death even to Mr Layton's invariably unnoticing eyes, because he actually frowned and gave her a second look as he handed her her key and asked whether she could do with a cup of tea. A whisky or five, thought Lindsay, saying, 'No, thank you,' and wishing she did have a bottle of 'the hard stuff' stashed up in her room. She would have drunk the lot, and then some, to wipe out the hideous night in a blind drunken stupor . . . pickle her brain into never remembering anything again.

Lindsay opened her eyes to the cold grey light of morning and felt worse than she had when she'd gone to bed. Every awful, humiliating moment came surging back with the first moment of consciousness that brought her out of the intermittent, uneasy dozes she had drifted into on and off during the night. She stared up at the ceiling and wanted to howl, and did cry a little from sheer self-pity, the stinging humiliation of it all—and for something lost . . . the prospect of Hugh's love and possibly a future together. Pure fantasy; the prospect had never existed outside her own adolescent imagination, Lindsay reminded her-self bitterly.

Kelly's scratchy clearing of the throat came a moment before her knock on the door. 'Lindsay . . .?' She followed up the knock with a raspy call.

Lindsay dragged herself out of bed to open the door, and then the shock in Kelly's eyes made her realise she must be looking as awful as she felt.

'You look awful. Are you sick, too?' Kelly whispered hoarsely.

Lindsay lied with a nod.

'Gee . . . both of us. How rotten,' Kelly commiserated with a sympathetic grin.

'I'm not really sick,' Lindsay had to admit grudgingly. 'Just a bad night. How do you feel today, Kelly?' she went on quickly, genuine concern mixed with selfish concern to distract Kelly away from questions. 'Do you mind if I don't tell about the exhibition just yet? I'm still a bit tired,' Lindsay added, thinking Kelly couldn't wait to hear about it and had hauled herself out of her sickbed at eight in the morning to get all the details. Then she spotted the large, gaily patterned carry-all on the floor and frowned. 'Are you going somewhere?'

'Home. To mother. Where else?' Kelly gave a raspy chuckle.

Where else, indeed? thought Lindsay later after

she had seen Kelly off. Home to mother—every daughter's age-old solution to her problems, and the only solution in her own case; there simply wasn't anywhere else. Lindsay smiled wryly to herself as she pictured Maggie having a fit when she turned up unannounced, but in the end Maggie would be like every other mother in the world: concerned . . . caring—and biting her tongue off not to be curious.

It was just a matter of organising herself . . . spinning on sixpence, and she could be home in days. There was no question about leaving . . . leaving Ruytons; leaving London; leaving every place and every thing connected with Hugh Rydon.

Lindsay ran a bath for herself—the standard four inches of lukewarm water, and composed her letter of resignation—to Edwards, not Hugh Rydon—while she bathed. 'Regret I've resigned and please send my folio back' said it all, but later, back in her room, Lindsay turned the bald statement into a stiffly formal letter including an apology for lack of notice, a vague reference to having to return to Australia immediately, and a request that Edwards arrange for a courier to return the folio to her on receipt of the letter—at her expense, she had to add as a postscript at the bottom.

That took care of the letter, and then Lindsay cheated by persuading Maree at reception to telephone Ruytons and tell their switchboard operator to tell Edwards she wouldn't be in that day—or ever, only he wasn't to know that until he received her letter the next day, which she posted on the way to the bank to withdraw the money for the air fare home.

A travel agent was the next stop, and Lindsay walked out into the familiar drizzle with a ticket in her bag and a feeling of everything somehow having been resolved—the coward's way, albeit—home with her tail between her legs—but she didn't care. Bravado was something she couldn't afford if it meant staying in London and running the risk of coming across Hugh when least she expected it.

And she didn't belong here in this bustling, sophisticated city with its sophisticated shops . . . sophisticated men who cheated on their wives without a bat of an eye. Out of her depth . . . a little country bumpkin hanging on to her ideals and principles, and heaven only knew how fragile they were, almost crumbling at the first contact with real temptation. She wasn't going to stay around for the second brush. Not that there would ever be one—here or anywhere else—because she would be on guard for the rest of her life against the Charles and Hugh Rydons of the world. And every other man, for good measure, Lindsay decided bitterly over a breakfast of a roll and coffee in a department-store cafeteria.

Maree gave her a funny look when Lindsay returned to the hotel several hours later. Lindsay gave her a stony one back on her way to the staircase for yet another climb up the interminable flights. How many more times was she going to have to haul herself up them? Not many. She was booked to fly out on Monday; today was Thursday; that meant three more days . . . at how many times a day on average . . . ? Lindsay was still doing her mental cal-culations as she came around the turn in the staircase one landing down from hers and looked up to see Hugh sitting on the top step of the last flight up to her room.

She froze where she was and stared. Maree's funny look was explained. The wretched girl might have warned her, thought Lindsay, her first reaction pure fury at the receptionist's deviousness. What . . . ? After Hugh Rydon had plied his charm and asked her not to? Silly Maree would have cut off her tongue first.

Then the charge of fury lost itself in the mass of confusion inside her head as the messages her brain was trying to send her got completely scrambled . . . Turn around and run back down the stairs . . . scream at him with all the rage bottled up inside her . . . run up into his arms and tell him she didn't care he was married, she wanted him anyway. Lindsay didn't do any of those things; rooted to the spot, she just kept staring, until Hugh broke the staring match with a wry smile.

'I've been waiting for you for ages,' he told her, lightly, with all the casualness of Kelly saying the same thing. 'Where've you been? Shopping?' he tossed in like an old friend, flicking a nod at the department-store carrier-bag that had the new cashmere jumper she had bought on impulse on her way home—a going-away present to herself.

'Yes, that's right,' Lindsay replied, quick as a flash. 'To buy a ticket home,' she elaborated, with a stinging offhandedness, she thought, and had the satisfaction of seeing the fatuously friendly smile disappear from Hugh's face in a hurry. 'If you've come to say goodbye, I'll take it as said, so don't let me keep you another moment,' she added tartly, pleased and a little surprised at how in control she was after all, after those first few moments of numbing shock. Then, when Hugh sprang to his feet without warning, Lindsay took an alarmed, reflex step backwards, stumbled, and made a wild clutch at the banister to steady herself.

Hugh was down the steps two at a time, but made no attempt to touch her after the first quick lift of the hand that dropped back to his side as her face warned him to keep it off her arm. 'I always did think these stairs were dangerous,' he quipped, smiling tentatively into her frozen face, his eyes wary and watchful.

From close up, Hugh looked as tired and strained as she probably did, as if he, too, had spent a rotten night, and Lindsay was meanly glad of it, although she suspected his bad night would only have been due to frustration, not to say fury, that she had walked out on him—or rather that he'd had an attack of chivalry and had let her walk out before he . . . The picture whirled into her mind like a hurricane, and all at once she was standing half-naked in front of him again, the damned pendant nestling between her breasts. Lindsay dropped her eyes in a fluster, her face burning and her hand shooting up to the lapels of her coat. The next moment, she pushed past him and started up the stairs in a belligerent rush, like a bull at a gate, and just as ungainly.

Hugh came up behind her as she unlocked he
door, breathing down her neck, almost literally; h
was standing so close she could hear the angry
rhythmic breathing through his nose, if not actually
feel it. Lindsay didn't protest when he came in
because she knew that telling him not to wouldn'
make any difference and he'd come in anyway. Sh
dropped her bags on to the bed and went straight to
the window, standing with her back to him. It wa
the only place in the tiny room where she could stand
without having to look at him, unless she stood with
her face to the door, or beside the bed staring into a
wall—a little absurd even for these circumstances.

'Marry me,' Hugh barked behind her, and
Lindsay's mind went into a freeze of shock.

She had heard those words countless times in the
pathetically romantic fantasy that had been lodged
inside her head for weeks—not barked out at her
proposals were not barked in heart-warming
fantasies. For long, silent moments Lindsay jus
stared blankly out of the window before her mind
jolted itself back to reality—with alarm. Had Hugh
really said 'marry me' or was she going loopy . .
hearing things . . . ? Odd things happened to people
when they were under stress; had they started
happening to her?

'Did you hear what I said?' Hugh asked, sharply
'I said marry me,' he repeated in a growl this time
not a bark, and Lindsay thought she was going to
laugh.

Her wildest dreams could come true; Hugh would
divorce Natalie for her and they would live happily

ever after. You didn't expect that, now did you? Lindsay taunted herself bitterly, and wondered how she could have overlooked such a neat little solution as divorce.

'Lindsay, say something. And for God's sake look at me,' Hugh burst out, frustrated anger pouring out of his voice. 'I can't even see what you're thinking with your face turned away. Look at me,' he ordered, and Lindsay turned her face slowly to him, knowing Hugh couldn't read a word of its stony expression as she offered it to his puzzled stare.

'What is it, darling? Why are you like this?' Hugh sounded as much worried as puzzled.

Had he actually expected her to jump into his arms in ecstatic delight that he'd sprung an offer of marriage on her—subject to a few inconveniences like divorce, of course?

'It's because of last night, isn't it?' Hugh jumped to his conclusion with a grimace. 'For heaven's sake, Lindsay, I didn't rape you, so stop acting as if I did. I was angry, yes, I admit it, but you can't blame me for that,' he muttered, defensively. 'When a beautiful, half-naked woman gives you the come-on and then backs off at a hundred miles an hour . . . well . . . I'm only human.' He shrugged in surly embarrassment. 'And I had no idea—not in the beginning, anyway —that it was going to be your first time, or how scared you must have been.' Hugh smiled, tenderly, understandingly, and Lindsay wanted to thump him and yell 'Not, scared, disgusted, you big oaf!'

'I understand how you must have felt,' Hugh went on, understanding no such thing. 'Or at least, I did

later,' he amended with a dry smile, 'when I'd go
over my frustration and pique, and then I was glad
darling, really I was—am, that you're not the sort o
woman who goes in for affairs.'

Was that supposed to be a compliment . . . He wa
all but patting her on the head and telling her she'
been a good girl. Lindsay smiled saccharinely. 'Nc
mistress material, do you mean, darling?' she cooe
with venom.' And are you sure, darling, that yo
really want to go so far as to marry me just to get m
into your bed?' she ran on in wide-eyed, breathles
wonder as Hugh looked incredulous. 'I mean to say
"darling",' she inserted another one in quickly, 'I'n
so very, very obviously inexperienced, aren't I, s
how do you know I'll be worth the hassle of all th
inconvenience? Perhaps you should have sampled th
wares last night while you had the chance,' she hisse
at him, unable to keep up the mockery anothe
second, and thought Hugh was going to hit her.

He shot out a hand and gripped her hard by th
arm. It hurt, and Lindsay gave a yelp and tried t
struggle out of the grip.

Hugh tightened his hold more painfully. 'Wha
hassle? What inconvenience? What are you talkin
about, Lindsay? I don't understand a word of you
rubbish. I asked you to marry me—be my wife,' h
spelt out in a roar. 'Do *you* understand that?'

'Oh, yes, but for how long?' Lindsay shot back
trying not to be frightened of him. 'Until you get sic
of me—as you have of Natalie? And have you tol
her yet, by the way, that she's about to be super
seded?' The last sneer failed abysmally, becaus

Lindsay's voice shook so much. And she was shaken, too, by the bolt of realisation that for all her makiness, for all her anger, she had not said 'no' to Hugh's proposal. And wasn't going to say 'no'.

'That she's . . .' Hugh started to repeat, and couldn't finish. The ugly, mechanical-sounding laugh broke out of him, and then went on and on. He let go of her arm and laughed until Lindsay became alarmed.

Hysteria? Did men have hysteria, too? Should she try slapping Hugh across the face? And get slapped back . . . ?

Hugh's laugh wound its way down to a sort of a growling, chuckling noise. 'I don't believe it.' He clapped a hand against his head in a parody of being dummoxed, and then shook his head wonderingly. Lindsay kept her eyes on him warily. 'Dear Lord, I don't believe it. Let's see if I've got this straight—and no, please, correct me if I'm wrong,' he insisted with facetious earnestness. 'But do you actually think I'm a married man? That I'm married to Natalie?'

Lindsay gave a hurried nod, scared not to, because Hugh's forced levity didn't disguise the rage in his eyes.

'Then what, in heaven's name, do you take me for? A philanderer like Charles?' Hugh bellowed, suddenly grabbing her by both shoulders and shaking her like a rag doll. 'Have you any idea what you're implying about me?' He let her go, almost in disgust.

Lindsay gaped at him.

Hugh turned his back on her, his shoulders rigid with his fury, and Lindsay's own anger came sweep-

ing out of the shock that had momentarily stunne
her faculties to witlessness.

'Whatever I thought was no worse than yo
thought about me,' she shouted at the furious back
'So now you know how I felt like when you wer
gaily jumping to all your horrid conclusions abou
me,' she hissed into the granite face when Hugh spu
around at her attack. 'And what else was I suppose
to think when Charles said . . . ? 'Lindsay began t
justify herself, and was cut off with another bellov
from Hugh.

'Charles! I might have known that coxcomb woul
have something to do with it. So what did the littl
rat tell you?' Hugh demanded angrily, but the rag
had left his eyes and the violence was gone from hi
too.

'That she was your wife—Natalie . . . I . . .
thought that she was his . . . and Charles said abou
the pendant . . .' Lindsay got herself tangled i
incoherence and stopped. And what did it matte
now what Charles had said?

'When?' Hugh asked, quietly.

Lindsay shrugged. 'Last night. Just before th
end,' she muttered, and looked away.

Hugh put a hand to her chin and tilted her fac
towards him again. 'But you were going to make lov
with me anyway,' Hugh said softly. Lindsay droppe
her eyes. 'You wanted to, didn't you? Until yo
found you simply couldn't give your lovely self to
married man. So that's what it was all about,' Hug
murmured, and gave a faint smile as he took his han
away from her chin and put it around her shoulde

d then they both stood there, staring silently out
e window. Lindsay didn't know what to say, and
ugh didn't say anything.

'Lindsay, darling, how could you have hurt
urself like that?' Hugh asked, pained, after their
ng silence. 'Why didn't you just ask me? No, I
pposed you wouldn't . . . couldn't,' he answered
s own question. 'Any more than I could bring
yself to ask you straight out about Charles. People
e so damned pig-headed when they're in love,
en't they?' he laughed, only half amused. 'Natalie
d I were divorced four years ago,' he went on with
sudden sharpness as if the subject was distasteful to
im. 'And yes, she does have a fancy for the name
ydon, and has reverted to using it again since her
st marriage broke up. I believe she thinks it has
ore status than the Snell she acquired from her last
usband,' Hugh explained sourly. 'And there's only
ne thing more important to Natalie than status, and
at's money, which is why she has the unpleasant
abit of descending on me in a hysterical flap from
me to time, convinced Ruytons—i.e. me—is
eating her out of her just dividends. She conned a
rge parcel of shares out of me in the divorce
ttlement. A small price to pay in the long run,'
ugh muttered under his breath, perhaps to himself.
e looked at her sharply. 'We were married for just
nder two years,' he told her almost angrily. 'Does
at give you an idea of the sort of marriage I had?
nd even then, Lindsay, if I had been reduced to
aving affairs, do you really think I'd have been so
bvious about them . . . ? He curled his hand around

her neck, and smiled, a little bitterly. 'You're
innocent darling, or you would have realised th
married people don't come on as obviously as I c
with you. They sneak about behind their partne
back . . . they arrange clandestine meetings and go
places where there's no risk of coming acro
anybody who knows them. It's a devious, shab
road into somebody's bed, and I can't believe y
could have honestly thought I wanted to take y
along it.'

Was he talking about Natalie? The bittern
sounded born of a first-hand knowledge of the w
married people went about their affairs. Linds
didn't want to ask, or know. What she did kno
though, was that there had been nothing devio
underhand about Hugh's attentions towards her. I
had made no secret of their dates; he had picked I
up at the hotel, taken her home again, called her
Edwards' phone; taken her to meet his friends at t
pub, taken her to his own home. Yet all it had tak
was Charles' malicious distortion of one fact
throw her mind into a loop and send it haywire w
instant distrust. Lindsay bit into her lip as the sha
crept through her.

'I was going to say you should know me bet
than that, but you don't, do you?' Hugh gave I
shoulder a squeeze. 'And that works both wa
neither of us knows the other very well.' Hugh w
only voicing what Lindsay was thinking.

'I'm sorry,' she mumbled, for her side of t
misunderstanding that had almost cost them th
future together.

Hugh laughed suddenly—a bright, happy laugh. 'Let's just say we're even, and forget it, shall we?' he suggested. 'We've a lifetime ahead of making it up to each other, and learning all about each other as we go along. You are going to marry me, aren't you?' Hugh's voice sounded worried, but his eyes were smiling, unconcerned.

Lindsay nodded. 'Yes, please,' she answered, primly polite, and made Hugh laugh again.

'Right,' he said briskly.' Then I'll have to get things moving . . . organise your papers from Australia . . . bring Maggie over. Anyone else you'd like . . . ? No more than a dozen, mind; I'm not going to have my house taken over by a contingent of Aussie squatters,' he told her teasingly. 'Oh, and we'll have to get you an engagement ring, since we're going to do everything by the book. Know any good jewellers?' Hugh was like a schoolboy on holiday. Lindsay had never seen him so happy.

She laughed up at him, and remembered something. Her face fell and, instantly, real concerned sprang into Hugh's eyes.

'Lindsay, what is it?'

'My resignation! I posted it earlier this morning—to Edwards,' she wailed.

Hugh's eyes cleared as quickly as they had clouded. 'Is that all?' he laughed in relief. 'Good grief, you really had me worried there. Relax, darling. I can assure you Edwards is the original soul of discretion and will pretend he never received it when you turn up at work tomorrow morning.'

'This afternoon,' Lindsay corrected, and meant it.

For a moment, Hugh's eyes looked as if he had other plans for her, then he shook his head at his own, very predictable idea. 'We've all the time in the world, I know, but darling, I love you so much I'm not sure I'll be able to wait until after I slip that wedding ring on to your finger,' he told her with a raw, throbbing longing in his voice.

'In that case, do you think you could manage to wait until you've slipped the engagement ring on to my finger . . . tonight?' Lindsay murmured happily as she snuggled deeper into Hugh's arms.

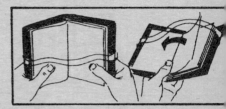
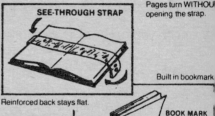

Janet DAILEY

THE MASTER FIDDLER

Jacqui didn't want to go back to college, and she didn't
want to go home. Tombstone, Arizona, wasn't in her
plans, either, until she found herself stuck there en route
to L.A. after ramming her car into rancher Choya Barnett's
Jeep. Things got worse when she lost her wallet and
couldn't pay for the repairs. The mechanic wasn't
interested when she practically propositioned him to get
her car back—but Choya was. He took care of her bills and
then waited for the debt to be paid with the only thing
Jacqui had to offer—her virtue.

Watch for this bestselling Janet Dailey favorite, coming in
June from Harlequin.

Also watch for *Something Extra* in August and *Sweet
Promise* in October.

Harlequin Superromance

**Here are the longer, more involving stories you
have been waiting for . . . Superromance.**

Modern, believable novels of love, full of the complex
joys and heartaches of real people.

Intriguing conflicts based on today's constantly
changing life-styles.

Four new titles every month.
Available wherever paperbacks are sold.

SUPER-1

HARLEQUIN Temptation

Give in to Temptation! Harlequin Temptation

The story of a woman who knows her own mind, her own heart . . . and of the man who touches her, body and soul.

Intimate, sexy stories of today's woman—her troubles, her triumphs, her tears, her laughter.

And her ultimate commitment to love.

Four new titles each month—get 'em while they're hot. Available wherever paperbacks are sold.

Temp-1